The Battle for Princess Madeline

Kirstin Pulioff

THE BATTLE FOR PRINCESS MADELINE
Book II of the Princess Madeline Series

Copyright © 2012 Kirstin Pulioff
Edited by Quill Pen Editorial Services
Cover Copyright © 2014 Elizabeth Mackey Graphics
ISBN-13: 978-1503213036
ISBN: 150321303X

Second Edition
Visit the author's website: www.kirstinpulioff.com

DEDICATION

Dedicated with love to my family.
To Chris, my very own knight in shining armor… and
Adeline & Tommy, who remind me to dream big!

CONTENTS

PROLOGUE—THE QUEEN'S CHOICE

"Eleanor, you have to choose."

"Why? Please tell me why." Eleanor's big green eyes pleaded with him.

He frowned, sighing and straightening his beard. His voice softened. "You've seen the mirror. You know what's at stake."

"That's not fair. That's not a choice." '

"You have a choice; there's always a choice. It's just not always an easy one to make." He looked down at her quivering lips and lifted up her chin. "The fate of the kingdom rests on your shoulders. Your tiny little shoulders." He sighed.

"But I don't know him, and I don't love him."

"My dear child," he said, "you will know him. Theodore is a great man and a good king. But it is your decision." He stepped away, dropping his arms.

"I want to see the mirror once more before I decide," she demanded, fire in her eyes.

"Of course, whatever will help you," he agreed, leading her from the room.

A small contingent of wizards led Eleanor to the mirror, a crescent-shaped pond secluded in the mountains east of the kingdom and guarded by a grove trees. It took three days of hard riding to reach the secret location, giving Eleanor ample time to recall her first visit there a few weeks earlier.

The images played over and over in her mind. Her uncle had taken her there to help her decide by giving her a glimpse of the future. Sitting on the shore's edge with her legs tucked underneath her, she had dipped fingertips into the cool water and asked to see her path. The ripples had grown.

Her first vision appeared, a memory of her family picnicking in the forest. Her parents smiled as she ran by with bouquets of spring blossoms, the soft petals blowing into the wind as she picked them off one by one. That was before the accident that took their lives, leaving her in her uncle's care. The water shifted to show her the upcoming royal ball. She was dancing with a man, the young king. Her eyes twinkled, and she laughed as they twirled. The last grouping of images filled her with dread. In her arms, she felt the weight of her children: twins, a boy and a girl. They were both beautiful, with piercing green eyes that matched hers. In their eyes loomed a green dragon. The image faded to black.

That was it. A grouping of three visions to decide her future. Her uncle reminded her it was her choice, but he was pushing for a decision. She was only fifteen, hardly a grown woman. She wasn't sure what she wanted. But the royal ball was approaching.

At last they arrived. Eleanor stopped her companions at the edge of the trees. The vision was hers alone.

Making her way quickly and quietly to the lake's

edge, Eleanor knelt as before, her soft gown tucked under her knees as her hands dipped into the cool water. A chill ran through her body as the water dripped off her fingertips. She took a deep breath, feeling a moment of peace amidst her anticipation. The trees rustled as she waited. Then, "I'm ready."

The wind blew her hair back as her reflection began to ripple. A soft ringing made her sit up straight.

"Are you ready?" she heard whispered back in the wind.

Eleanor jumped. Her heart started pounding, and she glanced around, making sure no one had followed her. No one was there. Just herself, the trees, the rocks, and the lake. She looked back at the mirror.

"You can speak?" she asked, leaning forward, her voice shaking.

"I can do all," it whispered.

"You haven't talked before," she countered.

"No one has doubted before." The water stilled. "I showed you one path already. Here is another."

Colors and images appeared on the smooth surface, beginning the same way as before. The sweet memory of her family picnic came first, and then the ball. She didn't dance with the king, but stood off to the side, watching as he twirled with another girl.

The image faded and a new one formed. Flames, destruction, and terror burned in the waters before her. People she recognized faded off the lake's surface as she stared in agony.

"No. No!" she yelled. The pictures continued, clearer than she wanted to see, more terrifying than she wanted to believe. "Make it stop," she pleaded, tears streaming down her face.

Her companions heard her cries for help through the trees and darted out to meet her.

"Take me back. I must see my uncle," she ordered with a quivering jaw and tear-stained eyes. The men led her back to her horse, and they rode as fast as they could back to the kingdom.

She found her uncle sitting quietly on her bed. Eleanor ran into his open arms and sobbed.

"Have you decided?" he asked at last.

"I have," she replied, wiping the final tears away with the back of her hand. "I will do it. I will become the queen."

"I found this for you, among your mother's things," he said, holding out a beautiful green silk gown, with gold embroidery and pearl accents.

Eleanor smiled as she held the soft silk. "It's beautiful, but green?"

"Yes," he chuckled at her. "It's what we wear," he said, pointing to his own robe.

"Yes, Uncle," she whispered. "Thank you."

"Our kingdom thanks you," Elias said, turning to walk out of her room.

CHAPTER ONE

"Princess Madeline?" her professor called. "Princess Madeline!" he yelled, whipping his willow branch on her desk, shaking his head. "Please pay attention. In the ancient days of the dragons, Lord Hawthorne created what we call 'Hawthorne's Theory,' a series of complex battle maneuvers designed to startle the enemy and keep them off guard," he continued, pointing to diagrams on the wall.

Princess Madeline could barely keep her eyes open. She was waging a personal battle between fighting off sleep during the day and fighting off her nightmares at night. Her eyelids grew heavier the longer Professor Warren spoke. The low, steady tone of his voice, the long lectures on lords, kings, and history, and even the bland beige robe he wore lulled her to sleep.

It wasn't Professor Warren's fault. He was doing the best he could to manage the thin compromise between King Theodore and Princess Madeline.

Earlier that summer, King Theodore had reminded Madeline of her royal duty and pressured her to marry. Outraged by his plan, she devised her own—defying him and running away to save her freedom. After being captured and beaten by bandits and narrowly escaping, she realized that she belonged at home. She returned, and new compromises were reached. Every day since, she and her father had performed a calculated dance, each giving in a little and each taking a turn leading, still trying to figure out some of the quirks of their arrangement. Professor Warren fit right in the middle, faltering under the control of King Theodore and the stubbornness of the princess.

"…And that is why his theory is generally regarded as a fool's notion in the battlefield." Professor Warren turned around and squinted, rubbing his eyes with his forefingers.

"Princess Madeline! Pay attention!"

Jumping at the sound of his voice, she opened her eyes, reluctantly leaving her dreams of sunshine and birds.

"Princess," he sighed, "could you please explain Hawthorne's Theory to me?" Crossing his arms, he waited for a response.

Madeline looked down at her notes. Brushing a few loose strands of brown hair out of the way, she smiled. Her papers were full of sketches of herself and Daniel, rather impressive ones, too, for only a few hours of work. She scanned the rest of her notes, feeling the professor's eyes on her and hearing the tap-tap of his shoes.

Looking up, she gave him her most innocent smile. "Good Professor Warren," she said, batting her sparkling green eyes. "You speak of Lord Hawthorne as if he were the most innovative of our leaders. I always believed my father, King Theodore, was the most innovative. What are the differences between their techniques?"

Professor Warren looked like he wanted to cry. His fingers tightened their grip around his willow branch and his temples pulsed. Since she had posed her response as a question, he felt obligated to answer and continue with his lesson. Madeline's cheeks turned pink as she contained her laughter. An impish grin stretched across her face as he turned around to show her the differences.

She closed her eyes, concentrating on the warmth of the sun on her long brown hair and porcelain skin. With her slender build and royal upbringing, she epitomized the perfect princess—mesmerizing, charming, poised, and confident—though she was stubborn as an ox. Her chestnut brown hair draped her back in deep waves, and her emerald eyes were still closed to focus on her daydream for as long as she could.

Daniel filtered into her mind: his sandy blonde hair, the sweet way his bangs fell down over his gray eyes, and his gentle smile. His laughter filled her mind and ears: a deep, throaty laugh, full of playfulness and strength.

The laughter continued, and Madeline realized it was coming in from the window, not just her mind. Her eyes drifted over, watching the golden sunlight flood in.

She sighed and looked down at her notes and

drawings. Already forgetting the lesson, she traced her fingers over the figures of herself and Daniel. Earlier that summer, she had broken many hearts by choosing her knight champion, Daniel, to be her betrothed, instead of the eligible royals.

Her sigh must have been louder than she thought. At the same time that she turned her gaze toward the sunlight, her professor sprang into action. His willow wand cracked against the window. With one swift twist, the drapery closed.

"Now, we will continue," he said, looking down at her notes with a sigh of his own.

The throne room bustled with activity. With the rapid approach of the fall festival, the long line of farmers and villagers waiting to see the king wrapped around the grand hall.

The colorful outfits of the entertainers brought whimsy to the hall. A red tunic here, yellow and purple pants there—like festive flags blowing in the wind, the patterns moved and swayed with their steps. The warm aroma of freshly baked bread, herbs, and spices filled the air. The jingling of bells and tuning of instruments charmed the ears as the stewards checked and double-checked that all were in their correct arrangements. Even the clucking of hens fitted the clamor.

Every year around this time daily headaches burdened the king, reminding him of the price of planning this festival. The mixture of sounds from the hall and the weight of the crown pounded his head from mid-day on. The added importance of this year weighed on his mind. Just as King Theodore had his hand in the lessons for Madeline, he had other ideas for his son. This year served as an introduction to the more tedious occupations of leadership.

Madeline's twin brother, Prince Braden, shared little in common with the princess. King Theodore thanked the stars that his son was his serious child. He might struggle to keep Madeline's adventurous nature and stubborn spirit in check, but at least he knew his kingdom would be ruled by a steady hand when he was gone.

Adjusting his crown, King Theodore looked over at the never-ending line of colors, noises, and animals. With a smile, he waved the first person forward.

"How may I be of service today, good farmer?" he asked.

"Good King, my neighbor and I," he started, pointing a finger back toward another farmer in line, "we're both top sellers at the festival each year, me for my pumpkins and him for his squash."

"You, please come forward," the king directed, pointing to the other farmer.

A skinny man with a stained work apron and dirty pants with holes in the knees stepped forward. He bowed low to the ground and placed a basket, filled to the brim with squash, at the king's feet.

"Please, continue," the king said, waving his left hand and leaning his head onto his right.

"Your Majesty," the first farmer began, bowing. "We both are successful in our own respective specialties, but his field workers are claiming plants that are on my land."

"Not true, Your Majesty," the other jumped in. "The plants are on my land."

"Both of you claim the plants are on your land? Are they squash or pumpkins?" the king asked, raising an eyebrow.

"Neither," they said in unison.

"Hmm…" King Theodore looked at each one respectfully and scratched his chin. "Here's what we're going to do."

The farmer's eyes widened as they listened.

"Each of you is to prepare for the fair as usual—pumpkins and squash—your booths side by side. I also want you to sponsor a third booth together—for this mysterious plant. Those proceeds will be split between the two of you and me. Next year, be more careful marking off your crop rows. Next." He waved the farmers off and winked at Prince Braden.

Surprise passed over both their faces at the next person in line.

"Prince Paulsen. Welcome." The king stood, shaking his hand firmly. "This is a surprise. What can I do for you this morning?"

He sat back down and stroked his beard, his curiosity and eyebrows raised high. Prince Paulsen had not been seen in the kingdom since earlier that summer when Princess Madeline had returned.

Prince Paulsen was a noble from the southern territories near the Bay of Morengo, known for his charisma and well aware of it. He knew how to use good looks and pleasing manners to get what he wanted.

"King Theodore," he began, bowing enough to show respect but not so much as to ruffle his perfectly-coiffed hair. "Earlier this season, I vowed my services to you. I searched for the princess and risked my safety for hers. Upon her return, I went even further than my word and captured all the bandits of the forest. It took months, but they've all been rounded up." He flashed a smug smile.

"You have my gratitude. This kingdom truly values your valor and courage," the king said, bemused. Prince Paulsen stared back at him. King Theodore raised his palm to ask if there was anything else on his mind. The prince's striking blue eyes went flat, losing their twinkle in outrage.

"Your Majesty," he continued, "I am here to claim Princess Madeline's hand in marriage. Surely you recall our deal?" His voice got higher with each word. Snickers crackled through the throne room.

"Our deal, Prince Paulsen," the king began, sitting up straight, "was that *if* you brought home my daughter, *then* she was yours to marry."

Prince Paulsen's cheeks flushed with embarrassment.

"You see, Prince Paulsen, you did not bring her home, so you don't get her hand."

"But surely my work these past few months wasn't for nothing?"

"Of course not; our kingdom thanks you. We can all sleep better now, knowing we're safe." A twinkle flashed in the king's eyes as he held in laughter. He always enjoyed getting the better of someone.

Prince Paulsen glowered as the king waved him aside to call his steward forward. Leaning in, the steward whispered something into his ear.

"Perfect," the king said, clapping his hands together. "Thank you for your hard work." He turned to face the crowd. "Gentlemen," he said, addressing the people still in line, "an important matter has arisen. Prince Braden will answer the rest of your concerns." Prince Braden's head shot up, and he straightened at the mention of his name.

The king stood and left the throne room, leaving Prince Paulsen fuming as the line of farmers snickered, hiding their faces behind their hands.

"Next," Prince Braden called out.

Storming out of the throne room, Prince Paulsen's humiliation burned into rage. He stopped at the front gates of the castle, looking out toward the forest, where his men waited. Staring blankly ahead, he wondered how he was going to explain his failure to his men and the people of Morengo. Despite their hard work and his charm, he had lost his rightful reward because the king had let his daughter choose her husband on a girlish whim. Running his hands through his hair, he tried to find a way to exploit this in his favor, a way to take back what they had worked for.

Ideas formed in his mind as he watched the forest trees sway, remembering all the men he had captured. His face twisted. "She will be mine," he vowed under his breath.

CHAPTER TWO

When Professor Warren agreed to take on mentoring Princess Madeline, he had only thought about the high honor and prestige of the task. Unfortunately, teaching Princess Madeline created unexpected problems. He did not anticipate an unending flow of antagonistic questions and a stubbornness to fight for her views on history. The princess was not like his former pupils. He wasn't sure if he was grateful for the challenge or grateful that he was on a first-name basis with the apothecary, who provided excellent medicines for his increasingly frequent headaches.

"Princess," he groaned, rubbing his temples with one hand and holding his willow branch in another. "You are misunderstanding. There are reasons for these battles, reflected in the chosen strategy…"

Pacing back and forth, he found his momentum again. "Battles serve a purpose most of the time. When a strongly-held belief is challenged or attacked, battle is seen as a way of defending and increasing the faith in that belief. How strongly that belief is held determines how hard we fight and what strategy to take."

Madeline sat on the edge of her seat, her brow furrowed, contemplating the meaning behind his words. Not necessarily agreeing, but at least paying attention. "Professor, that's what I don't understand. If you're in a battle with someone, don't you want to win? Wouldn't you fight to win, regardless of what has been challenged?"

"Yes, you want to win, but sometimes you act more reserved or cautious. Winning is important, but you still need to protect your kingdom, your people, and your integrity. Some of the older battle strategies focused on an individual's bravery, baiting the other side into one-on-one combat. This often turned into self-sacrifice or ambushes, and the technique was abandoned. Today, we fight in groups."

Both their heads turned when a third voice entered their conversation.

"Interesting strategies, yes. Those are involved in leading a kingdom as well. Thank you, Professor Warren." The king walked into the room and motioned for his steward to close the door behind them.

It was rare that he interfered with her lessons, though he frequently listened at the door for a moment or two. Madeline and Professor Warren shared a look of surprise.

Sweeping his crimson velvet robe behind him, he walked over to the window and pushed the drapery open. The soft breeze rustled through his hair and the warm sunshine snuck into the room.

Professor Warren's face reddened with embarrassment. Princess Madeline sat still, her arms folded onto her desk, hiding the sketches that had kept her busy for most of the lesson.

"Such a beautiful day, isn't it, Professor?" King Theodore asked mischievously.

Professor Warren nodded in agreement, stammering and adjusting his wand. Nervous tension built in his stomach and sweat beaded on his temples.

King Theodore turned his head to look up at the teacher with a smile, still holding onto the windowsill. "Professor, why don't you enjoy the sunshine today? I will continue Madeline's studies this afternoon."

Neither the professor nor Princess Madeline knew what to say, but Madeline didn't wait for more instructions. As confusion and relief washed over the professor's face, Madeline glowed. Closing her notes quickly, making sure her drawings were still covered, she stood up and walked to her father's side.

"Ready?" the king asked, holding his arm out.

They left the room quietly, leaving Professor Warren scratching his forehead.

Her skin tingled in the sunlight. They walked from the center of the castle across the courtyard to a tower that stretched to the sky. Madeline stole a quick look over her shoulder and smiled at Daniel. He stood by the wishing fountain, helping organize and direct the long line of farmers and villagers who were here to see the king. She watched him laugh and hand some dropped juggling balls to an entertainer. She chuckled as the balls escaped Daniel's hands and fell into the fountain. He beamed as his eyes found hers.

Her father pulled her arm forward, twisting her head around.

"Have you ever been to this tower before?" he asked.

She looked up at him, eyes twinkling. "Of course not."

The castle towers were considered off-limits, so naturally Madeline and Braden had tried to explore them since they'd learned to walk. They'd climbed the castle from top to bottom, playing games, sharing adventures and misdeeds, and growing familiar with every room except the towers. They had always been locked, sealed off from the young royals.

"Are we going up there?" she asked, too quickly to hide her eagerness.

"Yes, my dear, we're going up there," he replied, smiling. His voice sounded happy, but his eyes were guarded.

Her heart started to pound, excitement building as she held her breath, waiting for the click of the key turning in the door. When the door finally opened, she ventured a breath, only to inhale a whiff of stale air.

King Theodore grabbed a torch and started up the steps, leaving Madeline below, looking up into the dark spiral of stairs above her.

His footsteps quieted to a soft *tap, tap, tap* as she lingered below. Wonder filled her eyes, and her fingertips swept across cool cobblestones. A smirk grew on her face as she felt dust and dodged cobwebs. The magic of the tower unfolded around her. She had always imagined this tower as a hidden fortress, full of secrets and treasure. Now those secrets were unlocking all around her. Lost in thought, she heard her name.

A small wave of light flickered from the torch above. She imagined her father's furrowed brow as he wondered what was taking her so long. Madeline lifted the bottom of her dress and ran up the dark spiral.

The light dimmed and the air thickened as she approached the top. Slivers of light shone through boarded windows, highlighting the tower room's hidden treasures. Madeline's heart raced as she looked around open-mouthed. She thought she caught a glimmer in her father's eyes before he turned away.

Her father rarely showed his emotions, and Madeline didn't want to press the issue.

"What is this room?" she asked, trying to take in every feature of the dark, dusty chamber.

"This room," her father started to say. "This room," he repeated, pausing to open the shutters before leaning against the wall. His eyes stared past her.

"This room was what, Father?" Madeline pushed, not understanding his strange behavior and the depth in his eyes as he looked at her.

He looked back down at her and smiled again. Pushing the velvet sleeves of his robe up his arm, King Theodore continued, "This room is yours."

"What?" she asked. "This is mine?" Her voice squeaked as she spun around to take it all in again, seeing it anew.

"Yes," he answered, trying hard to hide the shakiness of his voice and the tears welling up in his eyes. "This room was originally your mother's, and now it is yours."

Madeline looked around her, taking in her new surroundings but also giving her father some space. She had only seen him cry once before, the day she had returned after he thought she'd been killed, and she wasn't ready to see that again. A king or prince or princess had to be strong and unrelenting, providing the stability, strength, and encouragement the subjects needed. Raw emotions were kept secret, and displays like this discomforted them both.

The sunlight peaked in through the window in rays of light, leaving the corners of the room shrouded in darkness. The chamber was still tidy. A bed was on the left side of the room, just out of the sunlight's reach. Green embroidered pillows were lined up against the back wall, a testament to hours of focused work. A wooden table stood next to the bed underneath a cobweb-covered candle, layers of dust blanketing what seemed to be a book. A golden figurine of a dragon leaning against the leather-bound book caught her attention, as did a single dried rose. Its white petals were dry but intact, as if time had simply forgotten it.

Madeline walked around, trying to imagine what

it was like when her mother lived in this room. What had she done during the day? What had she thought of at night before she went to bed? She sat down on the edge of the bed and crinkled her nose as a cloud of dust and dirt jumped into the air.

"Father," Madeline said, bringing his focus back to the present. "Why did she have this room? Didn't she have one in the center of the castle?"

"Yes, she did." King Theodore stroked his beard. "Your mother was more to me than just a wife and queen. She was my dearest friend and most trusted advisor." He leaned against the far wall as if a great weight was bearing down on him. "From the day that we met at the royal ball to the day that we married the following spring, we were inseparable. We weren't allowed to be together until the wedding, but we refused to be far apart, so Elias, one of my advisors, suggested this tower." His eyes glimmered.

He sat down next to Madeline. "We were so in love, but our wedding was delayed because my parents assured me that there were other practicalities to work out before it could take place. Your mother lived here so we could be close. I was never allowed up here. After we married, she wanted to keep it as her study and reading room, and I respected that. This is my first time here, too."

He paused and looked straight into Madeline's eyes, smiling. "I imagine that's where you get some of your stubbornness. Most women were not skilled in reading or articulating strategies—your mother, though, she was the best. She wanted to make a mark on the kingdom as much as I did. She continued to learn from Elias and her tutors and helped create the peace you see in the kingdom today. I never knew what she did up here, but this was her retreat, her escape, her study, and her refuge. It was a treasure to her, and I know you will treasure it too." He folded his hands in his lap and looked into her face, searching for something.

Madeline didn't know what to do or say. She had never been given something like it before. This was more than a gift; it was a memory of her mother, something to share with the past. She wrapped her arms around her father's neck and held on for a long time.

"Oh, one more thing, Madeline," he said. He moved her arms from around his neck and walked over to the window. "I wanted to show you your wedding gift." He guided her to a window, a childlike grin spreading across his face.

She stepped onto a pile of books by the window and peered outside. She gasped.

The view was breathtaking, the perfect panorama of the outlying countryside. She could see the village sprawling out below them, people wandering around like ants, the bright banners of the tournament grounds waving in the distance. The Blue Mountains spread to the east, and in the west the great forest loomed. Caught up in the beauty and silence of the world around her, Madeline found it hard to concentrate on her father's words. Tearing her eyes away from the landscape, she looked at her father, who paced back and forth, describing the different portions of the kingdom.

"As you know, there are four distinct regions in the kingdom. The great forest is to the west, the exiled lands and deserts to the east, the dragon's lair and the bay to the south, and Dragon's Gate to the north, with many territories and palaces along the way."

Madeline nodded absentmindedly.

"Well, beyond Dragon's Gate is a small village and uncharted territory." Madeline stretched to see where he was pointing. The arch of Dragon's Gate was visible in the far distance against the horizon. It was said to be where the last dragons had hatched.

Madeline's eyebrows rose as her father continued talking.

"That area beyond Dragon's Gate is to be yours," King Theodore said, his face flushed with pride.

All she could do was look at him, then off in the distance, then back to him. Her heart felt heavy and too big for her chest. "Thank you, Father," she managed, though her words seemed small in comparison to his gift.

The warm breeze continued to blow over her face. Off in the distance, Dragon's Gate seemed to shine brighter, flickering as if winking at her.

CHAPTER THREE

The next two weeks slowed to a crawl. The anticipation of exploring Dragon's Gate raced through her mind every other thought. King Theodore had promised Madeline an expedition to explore the area as soon as the preparations for the fall festival were settled. Once the villagers were in order, they'd sort out their trip. That gave them enough time to explore and still make it back for the festival. It was a great lesson in patience for Madeline, but patience wasn't her strong suit.

Only Daniel knew the right words to say to make the time bearable, though even he lost that battle on several occasions. Their evenings were filled with long walks, hand in hand, as the last of the warm summer nights started to chill and the leaves began to show their autumn gold. Their dreams grew bigger as the days shortened. Her mind filled with visions of their warrior stronghold: towers, villages, fairs, and tournaments.

Professor Warren, meanwhile, moved their lessons to her new tower. She had determined to know the area backwards and forwards before exploring, and they now spent their time talking about geography, the history of Dragon's Gate, and engineering and architectural feats. She had never been so engaged with her lessons.

There were old stories of hidden maps, secret tunnels, magical treasure, and dragons. She'd heard about them since she was a child; now she had her chance to find out if they were true. What sort of area was she moving to? What adventures were in store for her and Daniel? Her desire to learn fueled her studies.

As summer faded and fall began, Madeline's focus began to dissipate. The fall festival was set to start in just two more weeks, and there was no news about their travels to the north. The brighter the leaves became, the shorter her patience grew. Her nightmares had become more persistent, and every day was more of a challenge.

Professor Warren was busy, deep in thought, the willow wand flying back and forth through the air as his small eyes scanned the maps in front of them. She couldn't concentrate, her mind catching on every sound. She raised her head, hearing footsteps on the cobblestones. King Theodore entered the room, and Madeline looked down at her notes before rising.

"Father," she said, standing to greet him with a curtsy, her velvet green dress sweeping over the floor.

"Madeline," he smiled. "Professor," he nodded, turning to greet him. "It's a beautiful day today, isn't it?" he said with a wink.

"Yes, Your Majesty it is," Professor Warren replied, closing his notes. "Is it too good of a day to remain indoors?" he asked hopefully.

"Of course, Professor," he said. "Enjoy the rest

of the day." Madeline watched their exchange with curiosity. She twisted her fingers, trying to keep from fidgeting with excitement. Her green dress swayed as her body twisted in anticipation.

"Madeline," the king said, turning to give her his full attention. "Dragon's Gate awaits us." Winking at her, he turned to walk down the stairs, holding back a mischievous grin. "Everyone is waiting downstairs. Take only the bare minimum. We will be traveling light for speed."

"But Father, what about…" she tried to ask.

"Daniel is already waiting with the rest of the group. I wanted this to be a surprise. Hurry!" He swept his robe behind him as he began to descend the spiral staircase.

"They are all waiting," she mumbled, looking around the room. That didn't give her nearly enough time.

Throwing her arms up in both frustration and excitement, Madeline shook her head and looked around, her smile growing as reality sunk in. Grabbing her leather satchel, she threw a few things in—simple travel clothes, a plain apron, a charcoal-colored wool coat for warmth, and a nice dress for the time in Dragon's Gate. Her other dresses ended up in heaps on the floor. She turned around for a final look at the room. It was a mess, but it was going to have to wait to be cleaned up—she was going to Dragon's Gate.

She tied her hair up high and tiptoed to her window. Dragon's Gate winked back at her from the distance. Throwing her bag over her shoulder, she ran down the stairs.

She immediately saw Daniel, her father, her best friend Sophia, and a small group of her father's stewards and guards.

She ran forward and threw her arms around Daniel's neck. He blushed and gave her a quick kiss. Madeline turned around when she heard her father clear his throat.

"Are we ready?"

"Yes, Father," she said with an innocent smile. He motioned to the waiting horses.

When everyone had mounted, King Theodore led the way out of the castle. Daniel exchanged an excited glance with Madeline before following him. Sophia shot her an annoyed look as she fumbled to stay on top of her horse. Her arms draped awkwardly around the horse's neck. They hadn't ridden much since Madeline had been thrown by her pony and broken her arm when they were children. As best friends, when Madeline gave something up, Sophia did as well. Madeline laughed at her friend, still clutching the horse's mane.

"Sophia," Madeline whispered, reaching out to touch her shoulder. "It's just like old times."

Sophia's eyes softened and she smiled back, remembering the hours they'd ridden together. "Yes, just don't get tossed this time," she said, adjusting her grip once more.

Their small group filed out of the castle grounds

as the wooden gates shut behind them. With a swift kick, Madeline's horse jumped, and they were off.

Brammus kept low on top of the roof. His short, stocky body blended in with the village as he moved from house to house, camouflaged by his brown cape and light straw pants. Holding his breath, he squinted away from the harsh sun, trying to take in everything. He swore under his breath, not sure why he had been chosen for this chore, tracking the princess. It wasn't as if she went anywhere, or at least she hadn't until now. He had gotten used to sitting all day. Looking over his shoulder and taking care to remain unseen, he slid down the last thatched roof and ran through the wheat field to his horse.

They were heading north. He wasn't sure why, and he didn't care; his orders were to watch and report. Grunting, he kicked his horse to follow, careful to stay far enough back to avoid detection but still close enough to provide a detailed report of their movements. She had become Prince Paulsen's obsession, and he knew better than to upset the prince.

They rode swiftly for the next two days, the landscape changing as they made their way north. The rolling hills of Soron gave way to dry flatlands, the trees sparse and spread out. Each day Madeline discovered new things: the leaves were smaller, the greens darker, the air drier and spicier. Each evening,

Madeline slid off her horse into Daniel's waiting arms, the warmth of his embrace erasing the pain of riding all day. The night's ritual began, with stewards pitching tents and guards encircling the camp, making sure the location was secure.

Sophia hobbled around rubbing the back of her legs, her forehead furrowed and a frown on her lips. Madeline walked over to her friend.

"How are you holding up?" she asked with concern.

"I'm fine," Sophia sighed, slumping down on the log next to them. Her red hair was bundled up in a knot on top of her head, her riding dress smudged and dirty. "I didn't think riding was this tough," she admitted, picking stray leaves from her tangled tresses. "I don't know which has been worse: sleeping on the ground or riding that thing," she said, pointing to the wide-eyed horse in their makeshift stable.

Smiling, Madeline sat down next to her. "I know, but at least we're almost there," she offered. "Can you imagine how great this is going to be for us?" Madeline's eyes glazed over as her mind filled with adventure.

"Us?" Sophia asked, "You mean for you and Daniel?"

"Well, Daniel and me, of course, but you'll be here too. I'm starting a new life up here. I'll need my best friend at my side," Madeline said, reaching over to hug Sophia.

Sophia looked down at her toes and wiggled

them around.

Madeline sighed and turned to look for Daniel, who was still helping to secure camp. The stewards had camp preparation down to an exact science. Fire here, tents there, horses beyond. Madeline's mouth watered as she smelled something cooking. Her stomach growled. She hadn't realized how hungry she was until she smelled food.

Daniel was hunched over near the fire, putting the final pieces together on the tents—a few ropes to keep them secure for the night. While the knights and stewards slept under the stars, the king and ladies needed tents for their comfort, security, and privacy. Daniel's rough and calloused fingers worked on the knots, his fingers surprisingly nimble as he completed the intricate lacing. Her stomach fluttered.

Daniel turned to wave at her, almost as if her thoughts and feelings were audible. Heat flew to her cheeks.

Sophia cleared her throat to get her attention back.

"Sorry," Madeline said, blushing. "You know how it is," she said with a small smile.

"Yes, I do," she replied, giving her a small wink of understanding. They both laughed, watching as the rest of the camp came together.

As the sun fell beneath the horizon, they found themselves surrounding the fire pit, enjoying the atmosphere as the embers flew above the fire. The crisp air cooled them as they settled in for the evening.

Her fingers entwined with Daniel's. A special warmth seemed to surround them, something more than the heat of the fire. Madeline felt her cheeks turning crimson.

At last, they had reached the place where her future was going to unfold. Snuggling her head back against the crook of Daniel's arm, she closed her eyes. It was close to sunset, but in her mind, she could still clearly see the land. Dragon's Gate still lay north. It would be another day of traveling until they were there, but they were close enough to learn the weather and landscape. The territory was sandwiched between the boundaries of Prince Alleg to the northeast and Prince Morgan to the northwest.

The northern territories were a sight to see. The dirt was a deep red, rusty color, and solid as stone. Its dry surface was shot with cracks, making room for little patches of grass that had somehow found a way to grow. A rainbow of unfamiliar wildflowers bloomed, and the scent of rosemary filled the air.

Besides the occasional crackle from the fire, all was silent. Madeline sighed, lost in her thoughts. Daniel held her protectively, his eyes closed.

"Alright," the king said, rubbing his hands together over the fire. "Time to make our plans and get some sleep. We'll only have a short time before we must return for the fall festival." He stopped and looked at Madeline, seeing her face fall at his words. "I know you'll want to stay longer—but we have to get back. The seasons change more quickly up here, and there's still more to do at home before the festival begins. This might be the first year we celebrate the festival with snow."

Princess Madeline pouted but knew he was right. Looking at the horizon, she saw the snow line was already low on Dragon's Gate. That gave them perhaps a week until it hit their kingdom.

"We can review the maps more though?" she asked eagerly, hopeful to hold onto anything she could.

"Of course, my dear," the king replied. "I trust you—" he stopped mid-sentence, hearing a twig snap and a rustling in the woods behind them. He paused, listening, and a muffled cough sounded from the woods. "Madeline—hurry, get inside," he whispered, pointing to their tent.

She ran, pulling Sophia with her. Huddling close together, they sat still, listening to the silence and their own heartbeats.

"What's going on?" Sophia whispered, her voice trembling.

"I don't know," Madeline answered.

Outside, Daniel crouched low behind a tree, sword drawn, ready to attack.

The king's men gathered together, a small group surrounding the princess's tent and all the other's lined up with Daniel.

Daniel raised his hand up and counted down

with his fingers. He dropped his arm and they charged forward, jumping over bushes to find the hiding intruder.

Branches crashed in the distance as a man dropped down from a large tree. He bolted through the bushes and over the boulders.

The knights ran like hounds, but by the time they reached the man's position, he had disappeared. They panted as Daniel rested his head in his hands, his blonde hair waving in the wind.

"Sir," one of the knights yelled, lifting a piece of parchment from beneath the tree. Daniel ran over and looked at what the other knight had found. His eyes grew large as the color drained from his face.

"Sir Daniel?" the other knight asked.

"We have to go," Daniel said, already turning to run back to camp. He clutched the parchment, his knuckles wrapped protectively around it until they reached the king.

King Theodore read it and looked at him solemnly.

"Men, we need to break camp. We're being followed."

Camp broke in record time. Within a few minutes, they were ready to go. Madeline and Sophia waited on their horses as the final pieces were loaded. Sophia's eyes darted around her, and she jumped at every sound, making sure no one was watching her. Madeline was fuming, her cheeks red, her teeth clenched as all evidence of their camp was torn down.

"Why? Why do we have to go back?" she demanded, refusing Daniel's attempts to appease her.

"Princess," he said patiently, "we have to go because of what we found. I am your knight champion, and I have sworn to protect you. We must return to the safety of the castle." He slapped her horse on the backside, sending her off before she could argue further.

Princess Madeline gazed longingly over her left shoulder. A full moon showed her a glimpse of the land of her future, and she breathed a sigh of resignation.

"I'll be back," she vowed.

CHAPTER FOUR

Sunrises in the Blue Mountains were a sight to behold. The reflection of light over the green trees and cerulean peaks, a reverberation of color through the morning mist, filled the world with splendor. Elias spent most mornings in a crouched position on a treacherous peak in the Blue Mountains, watching the sunrise with great anticipation. The cliff edges stretched fifty feet above the trees below, the perfect stage for the morning show.

He rose suddenly. Wind rustled the hair out of his face and fluttered his sparkling green robe. His strong, solid face masked the emotions running through his mind.

Without hesitation, Elias shot his arms up into the air and spun around in a circle faster and faster, until he was a blur of green. He listened to the faint words floating through the air, quieter than whispers. His arms dropped to his side and his legs slowed, trancelike. His lips parted and words started to flow as he conversed with the wind.

The wind slowed and his robe stilled at his side. He bent down to retrieve his walking stick and bundle of goods and began the walk back to their cave, shaking his head. The wizard's apprentices were running their daily errands as he came into view. With one look at their leader, they stopped still.

Elias felt the blood drain from his face, and the deep lines in his forehead loosen. His staff slipped through his clammy hands, and he clutched harder to hold onto his bundle. Without warning, his eyes closed and his knees gave way.

He vaguely felt a hand leading him through the village and into his home. His aide propped his body at his desk, placing a quill and parchment in front of him, ready to record the messages from the wind. His hands ferociously scribbled on the parchment the moment the door closed.

Opening his eyes, Elias adjusted to the dim light in the room. The candles had burned down to the stubs, and small wax puddles spilled out along the table. His fingers tingled as he opened and closed his hands, wakening his body. He closed his eyes tightly and reopened them, anxious to see the papers in front of him. He whistled as he shuffled through them.

Rolling up his green sleeves, he hunched over and got to work. Hours passed. Sweat rolled down his forehead and new wrinkles etched into his brow. Time stood still as his mind continued to absorb the written words.

The cave remained eerily silent. The Exiled all seemed to hold their breath, waiting, knowing that something big was happening. The sun set on another day, and Elias had not moved from his home.

The early morning sun sparkled off quartz as

Emmett transferred water from the wells to the fountain. As an apprentice wizard, Emmett maintained the wells and cleared the paths: the mundane tasks required to keep their village functioning. Today was no different. Walking between the fountain and well, Emmett multi-tasked, practicing his charms with one hand and carrying the water with the other. His left arm traced an intricate design in the air. Light sparkled from the tips of his fingers as he muttered the incantation to himself. Blowing light brown hair out of his blue eyes, he stopped. Elias stood in his doorway, parchments in his hand, his face a mask.

Emmett stumbled backwards, dropping his buckets of water as he ran to tell the others.

By the time Elias reached the fountain in the middle of the cave, news had spread and half of the villagers had already arrived. Averting his eyes, Elias shifted the parchments in one hand and touched the cool water with his other, watching as the ripples expanded. The circles in the fountain collided.

"Fellow wanderers," Elias said, pushing the hood of his green robe back to expose blazing eyes. "By now, some of you know that I have been in contact with the other side." A series of gasps ran through the crowd, and a few women knelt.

Undaunted, he continued, passion resonating in his voice. "It has been almost seventeen years since our exile. According to the news I just received, it seems the time has come full circle. We have waited, watched, and wished. I have seen what is coming, and we are needed. It will take our vision, courage, and strength. We will be tried, pushed to the edge of our endurance, but it must be so. Like ripples in water, we will return to the center, back to the beginning. We will be in exile no more!" Elias smiled as the people roared in excitement.

Elias didn't wait for the crowd to settle. Raising his right arm and his voice, he looked into their faces. "There is not much time. I will be leaving now with a small group, and the rest of you must be patient. We will all be together soon, but we must follow the signs. As it has been foretold, the time of the dragons is near," he said, shaking the parchments in his other hand.

His eyes surveyed the crowd, sifting through his choices and weighing each carefully. "You five," he said, his eyes fixating on the back corner where Emmett stood with his two older brothers and parents. "Come with me."

With a quick nod, they jumped into line and followed Elias. A rush of whispers ran through the crowd. The group walked to the opening, the voices of the people rising behind them. Green light erupted from the mouth of the cave.

CHAPTER FIVE

The sun set in the forest. No stars were visible through the green branches. The only sounds were Prince Paulsen's careless footfalls as he stomped through the leaves. He paced back and forth, anger growing with each step as his scout bowed before him.

Red wrinkles marked his forehead, and he wore a fearsome scowl. Waving his staff, Prince Paulsen faced his scout.

"You what?!" he yelled, wanting to make sure he had heard correctly.

"I followed the princess like you requested," Brammus said, his voice and hands shaking violently. "You told me to follow and keep you informed of her position."

"I did not ask you to get caught! I did not ask you to give them reason to keep guard, and I most definitely did *not* ask you to take your time getting back to me! I heard the news from other channels before you made it back. Incompetence!" Prince Paulsen snapped. Brammus fell as the staff collided with his cheek, then his stomach.

Paulsen turned his back to his men and continued pacing, counting his steps as he concentrated on his next move.

Behind him, some of his other men ran to

Brammus and carried him off to have his injuries treated.

Prince Paulsen stood oblivious to it all, his hands moving a mile a minute, marking the air with the ideas running through his mind. Every once in a while, his men heard a yell or hiss, usually followed by a wild cackle.

His followers were split. The younger knights seemed entranced with the spectacle he was making of himself. His peers and elders shook their heads, unnerved by his new obsession with the princess. But they said nothing. The last time someone suggested that he was going mad was the last time that man had spoken.

Prince Paulsen paced for hours; brief moments of exclamation and excitement passed without notice. The camp remained quiet. They stoked the fire and waited for their leader to come back to his senses.

It was late into the night when his excited outbursts stopped.

"Men," he said, snapping his fingers. "Gather around! I have a plan." No one moved. "Men!" he screamed. "Gather round!" He waited as everyone scampered into position close to him.

His manic pacing began again. His eyes gleamed as he gazed into the fire, entranced by the dancing light.

"Listen," he started, a strange enthusiasm in his voice. "Last year, we performed a great service and were promised a great reward that would raise our kingdom's status and ensure our future. That reward was withheld from us. It's up to us now. Our territory must receive what is rightfully ours. We must retrieve it."

His men sat still, considering the tantalizing promises of wealth.

"We rid this forest of bandits, but now we need the riffraff's help. We need a mass of men to secure this reward. I task each of you with our goal. Bring me all the fighting men you can find. Offer gold, homes, a stake in our future. Our success depends on your success." He paused. The younger men cheered; the elders feigned joy.

"One week. Return to me in one week's time. By the first snowfall—we attack!" Prince Paulsen commanded, and his men roared in agreement. "The time is ours! The reward is ours!"

The forest seemed alive with action. With no time to waste, the men focused on their new goal. Camp broke as each man headed out to find the bandits again.

Prince Paulsen stood next to the flames, his eyes gleaming in the flickering light as thoughts of gaining Princess Madeline danced through his mind.

CHAPTER SIX

Elias's group hurried from the mountains toward King Theodore's castle. Clothed in their traditional green robes, they looked like little trees on horseback. Elias led them forward, his head held high, almost challenging the wind. They made good time, traveling with only the clothes on their backs and emergency supplies.

This was Emmett's first time away from the mountains. A strange exhilaration ran through him as he took in the new sights and sounds of the journey. His knuckles were white from clutching the horse's mane. They had horses at home, but he had never ridden one so fast or far. His heart pounded in rhythm with the horse's hooves. That excitement faded at the sight of the castle, and his apprehension grew.

They were on a mission to reach King Theodore. Emmett did not know much history—the older wizards didn't like to talk about it—but he knew enough to understand that whatever was going on had to be important to break the covenant of their banishment. When he was a small child, they had left, vowing to never return. Now they were rushing toward the kingdom, into danger. He tried to push his nerves aside. Whatever lay ahead, he planned to enjoy these moments of wonder, in case they were his last.

The castle of Soron was a bright beacon. Its tall towers, thick walls, and fluttering banners marked the horizon, both welcoming and warning its visitors. Slowly it grew from a speck in the distance to a monument that loomed in front of them.

Elias exhaled and pulled his lips tight. Raising his arm, he motioned for his group to stop. The ground shook below them as a contingent of castle guards approached, their horns blaring and their banners waving in all directions.

"Hold there!" The lead guard's voice boomed. His horse snorted, prancing in place as the reins were pulled tight.

The other guards kept a careful eye on the wizards, pointing the tips of their swords at anyone made a sharp movement. Whispers of treason and years of wild speculation governed the guard's thoughts.

The leader dismounted his horse and approached Elias, giving him a wide berth as he circled around him.

"I didn't expect to see you again, old greenrobe," the guard sneered with contempt. "What business have you here?"

"We request an audience with the king," Elias said.

"Oh, the king will want to see you," the guard said, the corners of his mouth turning upwards as he remounted his horse.

The other guards led the six wizards to the castle walls. Their horse's hooves echoed off the hard cobblestones at the castle entrance, announcing their arrival. Stares greeted them. The anger, curiosity, and fear in the people's eyes left a heaviness on Elias's heart as he watched a child peek from behind her mother's back.

You could cut this tension with a sword, Emmett thought.

The soldiers led them up the cobblestone pathway through the square and up to the castle gates. Elias pressed on, keeping his head high and strong. His shoulders had always borne the weight of leadership, even in his younger years as an apprentice. His natural skills developed early and he surpassed his peers, earning a position of power at a young age. In time he became the king's advisor. After the exile, his responsibility grew greater.

Although he had prepared for it, the reality of the scorn directed at his people felt almost unbearable. They hid their faces deep inside their green hoods, hoping to escape scrutiny. Pressing forward, step after step, they made their way to the main castle square. Word of their arrival had spread, and hundreds of faces crowded around them, trying to catch a glimpse of the wizards. It wasn't long before King Theodore emerged.

His red face spoke louder than any words could. This was not a friendly meeting. His stewards gave him plenty of space, stepping back as he bellowed his orders.

"Seize them at once!" he yelled. The sneer that appeared on his face cut deeper than the anger in his voice. In that moment, recognizing the pleasure the king took in his 'command, Elias knew he had his work cut out for him.

"Theodore, wait," Elias yelled, his voice strong.

King Theodore stopped in his tracks. The crowd did not know where to look; even Elias's group averted their eyes.

"Guards," King Theodore said, straining his voice to stay calm. "Please remind these people who I am as you take them to the dungeon."

He stepped forward to enter the castle, and his knights closed in on the wizards.

Elias knelt and bowed his head low. "King Theodore, great leader of the western lands, please hear me out." His plea hung high in the air. King Theodore paused for a moment, then continued to walk away, not looking behind him as the doors shut.

The six visitors kept their heads bowed as the knights clamped chains around their wrists and led them away into the depths of the castle.

CHAPTER SEVEN

The first step into the dungeon was the worst. The foul air that greeted them nearly knocked Emmett out. The old catacombs that had been repurposed into the king's dungeon brought back many memories. As Elias smelled the air, a smoky scent transported him back seventeen years.

This is where the wizards had trained, studied, become who they needed to be. Bright memories of potions, books, late nights, and excitement raced through Elias's mind. He let out a deep breath and sighed. All the bright, bubbly memories of the past faded, enveloped by the gray haze of disuse and dust.

There was little time to soak it all in. The guards removed the thick cuffs that left angry red marks on the prisoners' skin and slammed the door to their cell. Emmett and his family crouched against the back wall, trying to calm their mother's flood of tears. Her body curled into a ball in his father's arms.

Her soft wails struck Elias's heart. He turned, wanting to reassure them. A new sound filled the air. Laughter. The strange cackle echoed off the walls, coming closer. Heavy footfalls signaled someone's approach. Elias's heart felt heavy.

"Elias," a voice echoed from around the corner.

Elias raised his head. "My king," he responded, kneeling on the cobblestone floor. Emmett's family glanced at the empty doorway, then at Elias. Emmett's mother quieted her tears, and the men knelt around her.

"You old fool," the king hissed, rounding the corner. "I knew you couldn't stay away." His eyes betrayed malice and amusement. He rubbed his beard, then leaned over and whispered something to the guard.

The guard's eyes opened wider as he held out the ring of keys. The wizards watched in bewilderment. Surprise and fear glistened in their eyes, hope throbbing in their chests.

"Get up, Elias!" King Theodore snapped, turning his back on the cell. "You can leave us," he said to the guard.

The guard bowed his head. "Yes, Your Majesty." He slipped out.

"Well, well, well," the king said, pacing back and forth, twirling the keys around his fingers. "I spared your life once and swore I'd never do it again." He stopped for a moment to stare at Elias, his face red, eyes tense. "Why have you broken our truce and returned to my kingdom? What is so important that you risk your life and the lives of your people? What excuse do you think will change my mind?"

Silence echoed between them as Elias looked up, formulating his response, feeling the weight of everyone's eyes on him. He hoped their faith in him was not misplaced. Wrapping his fingers around the iron bars of the cell, he looked into the king's eyes.

"Eleanor," he said.

In a single moment, Elias watched the king's face flicker from anger to pain, sorrow, and confusion.

"Eleanor?" the king repeated, steeling his gaze. "You came here for my wife? You're a bit late for that."

"She was my niece as well as your wife. You must know the truth." Elias held out his arms in a pleading gesture. "Theodore, please. Hear me out. I can show you something to ease your mind."

The king's back stiffened. "Again, kinsman," he sneered, "you remind me of your relationship to Eleanor. Let me remind you of something: She was my life. You let my beloved die. Seventeen years is not nearly enough time to cool my anger."

He let out a ragged breath and moved closer to the cell. "I will give you one more chance. Tell me why I should listen." He turned the key in the door. The cell opened with a loud clank.

Elias stepped forward and looked back to the other wizards. He smiled warmly and touched the bars. "I will be back soon," he said, his words calming the fear in their eyes. The king blocked the others from leaving and closed the door.

"All right, Elias," the king said. "Show me what you will. I have already given you more time than I had planned. I have other matters to attend to."

"It's in her tower," Elias said simply.

They walked from the dungeon to the tower,

taking the underground corridors to avoid being seen. Icy silence stood between them like a wall.

Elias felt tears well up in his eyes when they reached the base of the tower, memories of his love for Eleanor rushing into his mind and heart.

"This is Madeline's room now," King Theodore said, and a slow smile appeared on Elias's face.

They climbed quickly, Elias sure that the king's patience was wearing thin. It had always been in short supply, and he didn't imagine it had grown any while he had been exiled.

The room had stayed much the same. Princess Madeline kept the bed in the same position, only adding a few of her pink and rose pillows. The side table that had once been empty now overflowed with personal items—a mirror, a couple of books, a carved bird, and a green shell necklace. A large stool sat below the window, which boasted a panoramic view of the village, forest, and the far-off Dragon's Gate. An empty room kept as a tribute to Eleanor had blossomed into life under Madeline's care.

Elias wandered through the room, lost in his own thoughts—happy, wonderful memories of himself and Eleanor. With a deep sigh and a full heart, he sat back on the edge of the bed. He closed his eyes and pointed behind the chamber's entrance.

"Over there. There should be a loose block about knee-high from the floor."

King Theodore raised his eyebrows as he walked over to the doorway. Bending over, he brushed his fingertips over each stone. He jumped back as sand crumbled to the ground and a stone moved under his touch.

"Open it, my King. The proof you seek is inside." Elias waved his hand but stayed seated, pulling a roll of parchment out from under the cascading sleeves of his robe.

The king didn't hesitate. His hands moved with an urgency they hadn't known in years. The stone moved aside easily, an audible click sounding as the seal broke and a hidden compartment appeared in the darkness. He pulled out an aged leather package marked with Eleanor's seal and stifled a gasp.

Shaking, he sat on the floor, pulling the package up to his chest. His lips opened and he savored the remaining smell of Eleanor's sweet lavender perfume. Whatever it was, she had left it for him to find. He placed the package back on the floor to open it.

Choking back a sob, King Theodore read aloud, "My beloved husband." Tears welled in his eyes, heat filling his cheeks as feelings he had long forgotten rose back to the surface. "I had hoped this day would not arrive, but it has. We are coming into an age when the sleeping dragons will awaken. There is only one way I know to protect our children. Please love them, protect them, and prepare them for what is coming. I have loved you without limit. Always, Eleanor." He lifted the page to his face and sat in silence.

After a few moments, King Theodore turned his attention to the rest of the package—an encrusted pewter ring and a packet of age-worn papers. He fingered the ring and read the first few pages. Looking sharply up at Elias, he snapped, "How did you know of this?"

Elias knelt beside the king and rolled out the parchment that had been hidden inside his robe. "She sent me a message as well. I didn't read it until after you ordered the exile, and then…"

The majority of the parchment matched what King Theodore held. Word for word, picture for picture, map for map, they were exact duplicates of each other. Elias had a few additional papers that pinpointed where and when to find the king's copy, including a timeline showing events that had yet to unfold and cryptic references to the Dragon's Age.

"My King," Elias whispered. "We haven't much time. If these are correct, the time of the dragons is near."

"Yes," the king agreed, packing the materials together and standing. "We must warn Braden and Madeline. We can review these later."

He stretched his arm out in response. Elias clasped the king's arm in a knight's greeting. The green in his robe brightened as they turned to descend the stairs.

CHAPTER EIGHT

A buzz of anticipation hung in the air the week before the fall festival. Farmers rushed to ensure their final harvest schedules were aligned. Flowers and autumn bouquets hung from the shop windows, tempting the visitors. Bakeries filled the streets with the sweet aroma of freshly baked pastries to tease every sense.

The best part, Princess Madeline believed, was the harvest break. Studying and training always paused for several weeks to allow students, apprentices, and workers to help with the final harvest and preparations for winter. The younger knights assisted as well, their normal training duties cut in half. That freed up time for Madeline and Daniel to spend together.

The interior of the courtyard rang out with laughter as the children made off with all the sweets they could take. Loaves of bread and stems of flowers littered the streets behind the streams of giggling little ones. A few knight apprentices were in the corner showing young boys how to sword fight with sticks, jumping in and around the hay bales.

Having been released soon after King Theodore and Elias returned from the tower, Emmett and his family sat on the sidelines, watching the courtyard with wide eyes. Emmett tried to figure out how he might join in.

Princess Madeline basked in the sun. The weather had begun to change, and the air felt chilly whenever a breeze swept through the courtyard. But when the air stilled, the sun shone through her red velvet dress. Bluebirds chirped in the fountain beside her, enjoying an afternoon of splashing.

For a moment, they looked like a happy group. Princess Madeline leaned back into Daniel's chest. Sophia and Prince Braden were standing nearby, their hands close together, laughing at the frolicking birds. All was well until Braden brought up Madeline's studies and their argument began again.

"I still don't see your point, Braden," Madeline sighed. "If we're at war and you have your men lined up, do you attack or wait?" She sat up straight and crossed her arms.

They had been arguing for weeks.

Braden shook his head. "Madeline, I think you're taking your lessons too seriously," he said. "If the castle were surrounded, there are a couple of options. The king can demand a one-on-one duel to decide the outcome, the army can attack, or you can wait it out. In fall or winter, we'd wait it out. It's much tougher for the attackers to survive on the outside than for us to get by on the inside."

"But—" she protested, rubbing her temples.

"Madeline," Daniel jumped in. "It's much too nice of a day to worry about such things. That is what the knights are for, and we're always training for new situations."

Madeline pouted. "I understand that, but it doesn't feel like that's the right answer. I feel like my dreams are saying something different, like something new needs to be tried," she said, hands on her hips, eyebrows scrunched up.

"This is about dreams?" Braden asked, annoyance clear in his voice. "What kind of dreams?"

"Bad ones," Madeline said, looking up at her brother. "I've been having them for months now, ever since the summer. They feel so real..." her voice trailed off. "They're more than just dreams."

Daniel took her hand in his and rubbed his strong arms over hers in reassurance.

"It always starts the same way. I'm surrounded by white fog. I can't see anything, and yet I feel safe. I don't feel alone... sometimes I wander, trying to find a way out, and at other times I am guided. One thing is always the same, though—we have been attacked. As hard as it is to believe, in every dream we have been attacked and I have to react. It doesn't seem like these options we have been talking about will work. They're certainly not easing my mind. We've been learning about these battle strategies, and I'm just trying to find a way to solve my dream. I know it's silly."

"Well," Sophia chimed in, "what's silly is worrying about this. It's just a dream. We all have bad dreams sometimes. There's nothing to worry about. As you've always pointed out, King Theodore is a wonderful leader. He'll know how to act. He has a team of scholars at his right hand to create new strategies, the most gifted and loyal knights in the world, a kingdom of supporters, and a brave and charming prince." She smiled at Braden, who winked back. "Bravery and courage are in abundance. If anything, it is your lack of confidence that we should concern ourselves with."

Everyone stared at her. She continued, "Here we are on such a wonderful, clear fall day, and you're intent on spoiling it for the rest of us. Stop being so self-absorbed and open your eyes." Sophia stopped and covered her mouth, surprised at what she had said.

The group was speechless. Braden and Daniel looked at each other and tried not to laugh, while Madeline's cheeks grew red.

"I'm sorry, Madel—" Sophia began.

"No, please don't apologize for speaking the truth," Madeline told her. "You're right, I do need to let this go. I'm worrying over a dream. Now," she said, glancing over at Daniel, then back to her friend. "Do you want to help me finalize some plans for the wedding?"

"Yes!" Sophia squealed, a smile exploding on her face.

The girls were safely secluded on one side of the fountain, giggling. Madeline's red dress and Sophia's flaming hair reflected off the fountain's surface, as bright as the banners of Soron. Their heads stayed close together, keeping their secrets hidden as they stole quick glances at Daniel and Braden.

The men had joined the sword-fighting knights. Daniel jumped on the bales, sending the kids roaring with laughter while Braden stood to the side.

King Theodore and Elias stood watching the group, knowing what they were about to stir up. Elias caught the eyes of the wizards sitting in the corner. A wave of relief flowed over him as he noted their ease.

With a sigh, Elias looked at Madeline and Braden and nodded to the king. King Theodore's smile faded as he approached the group, severity in his eyes. Braden saw them first and noticed the formality.

Standing and adjusting his shirt, he addressed Theodore. "Father, what is it? What's wrong?"

"Elias?" Daniel asked, recognizing the man who had helped him on his quest to rescue Madeline. "What are you doing here? I thought you were…"

"Exiled," the king said, finishing his sentence. "Yes, he is, but for now we are working together on a special matter." He looked around at all of them and continued. "Braden, Madeline, I am sorry for interrupting, but there is a troubling matter we must discuss. To my study, please."

Without hesitation, Sophia stood and curtsied, leaving the group to their plans. She glanced back once to see if Braden noticed.

"Such a polite girl," Elias said, winking knowingly at Braden. Braden coughed and his face turned red.

King Theodore led them in the direction of his study at a brisk pace, his face clear and hard as stone, his robe billowing as they walked. Madeline reached over and squeezed Braden's hand for reassurance. He squeezed back. Elias trailed, watching the siblings as they made their way into the castle.

Their footsteps echoed through the hall and up the stairs. King Theodore's study was a wonder, filled floor to ceiling with books, maps, tapestries, and curious items from his travels. His favorite artifact, a handcrafted model ship, rested prominently on the corner of his desk.

King Theodore cleared his desk with the sweep of an arm and unrolled the parchment that he had been hiding in the sleeve of his robe. "Your mother, was a wonderful woman, too wonderful for me," he said. Madeline and Braden's heads flew up. "She knew... strange things... and I found a special message she wrote for you two." He rolled the parchment out and stood to the side. Madeline and Braden rushed over to read the words.

Madeline read it twice to make sure she didn't mistake anything. Braden stood to the side with a deep scowl when he finished, his anger seething through his tightened jaw.

"I don't understand," Madeline said, looking back and forth between her father and Elias. Worry and wonder shone in her emerald eyes.

King Theodore pinched his lips together and

opened his arms to hold her, the rich velvet on his robe soothing her as she leaned into him. Elias explained, weariness and sorrow evident in his eyes and furrowed brow.

"Princess Madeline and Prince Braden, although this may not make sense right now, I need you to try and understand." He looked at them both and continued when he was satisfied that they were listening.

"Your mother was a very special woman. Extraordinary in all that she put her hand to, and it appears that she put her hand to more than I was aware of." He coughed to clear his throat before continuing. "You see, Queen Eleanor came from a gifted family of wizards, each member skilled in magic. Some members have chosen to develop these talents, and some have chosen to forgo them and focus on a more traditional life. There is no right or wrong choice, but it is a unique choice only available to those in our bloodline."

Elias's eyes continued to go back and forth between the two young people as he spoke. "That choice is usually made on your sixteenth birthday. Every person descending from the wizard bloodline must make that choice. If they forgo the magic and choose a traditional life, the magic leaves them, and their children do not have that option. When Eleanor reached her sixteenth, she chose circumstances that brought her to your father and her life as queen. I believed that she had chosen tradition over magic. I was wrong."

Elias leaned over the desk to point at the lettering on the parchment. "What your mother chose was this," he said. "Naturally gifted, she knew about events long before they took place. She has detailed some of them here," he pointed to the cryptic phrases, "and some, we may never interpret."

"What do you mean?" Madeline asked.

"Your mother knew that the age of dragons was coming, and that we needed powerful magic to win. In her last breath, she wove a spell to give each of you, if you chose the path of magic, half of her skills on top of those you were naturally born with. She knew that something was coming, and that her sacrifice was the only way the kingdom could survive. Now comes the tough part," Elias said, searching each of their faces in turn. "You both have already passed your sixteenth birthdays, in the summer. There was no way for your father to know, to prepare you, or to let you know what your options were. Neither answer is wrong, but we need to know." Elias dropped both hands on top of the desk. "The morning of your sixteenth birthday, what did you choose? Did you choose the path of magic or the path of duty?"

Braden jumped up. "How dare you, a stranger, an exile, pry into our personal choices?"

"Braden," King Theodore said, still holding Madeline close. "That's enough. This man has every right to ask you. He was one of my closest advisors."

"But Father," Braden pleaded. "He is an exile. He let our mother die. Why should we believe him or answer his questions? He knows nothing about us."

"He knows more than you think. Please answer the question. He is here to help."

"Father, I don't understand. This man is our enemy. I'm not going to trust him with my life, my feelings."

Elias stood back and watched the fireworks between the two of them, noticing their similarities. Braden was a mirror image of a younger King Theodore.

King Theodore saw the confusion and anger in his son's eyes. There was only one way he would relent. "He is not our enemy," the king began. "He is your uncle. Now, please, think back, this is very important. What was your choice?"

Braden looked up at his father. He pulled himself together. "I didn't choose it, Father. I chose to follow in your footsteps." Both King Theodore and Elias lowered their eyes.

"I didn't know, Father, I didn't know," Braden said, his face pink with embarrassment and regret.

"Madeline?" King Theodore asked, holding her away from him so he could see her face, searching for a different response.

All eyes were on her. She felt the weight of their hope. Her mind began to spin as she looked from eye to eye, face to face. The color drained from her as her eyes settled on Elias. "I chose our mother," she said.

She collapsed in her father's arms.

She drifted into the dream, a thick white haze in front of her, guiding her forward. Lifting the hem of her white dress, she ran, as fast and as far as she could. A voice whispered her name, "Madeline, sweet Madeline." She turned to the side and caught a glimpse of something green and sparkling fading into the forest. She ran deeper into the fog, trying to catch it, feeling eyes following her. She didn't stop until a thick fog surrounded her, leaving her alone but not afraid.

Elias, King Theodore, and Braden all knelt beside the princess, calling her name. They didn't notice the snow starting to fall in the courtyard.

CHAPTER NINE

A light mist floated above the ground and beneath the forest trees. An eerie quietness clung to Prince Paulsen's camp, as if the mist had blanketed his men's minds.

The sun went down and the crickets were chirping as Prince Paulsen began pacing. The air grew cooler and the tension thicker as he looked each man in the eyes, terrorizing each in turn. The men tried to remain calm, to appear tougher than they were. Hours passed while the silence grew, more intimidating than any words could have been.

Prince Paulsen scratched his chin, reveling in both the feel of the rough skin under his fingertips and the appearance of the group in front of him. In one week's time, he had gathered an army to fight for him. *Maybe not the King's Knights,* he thought as he watched one of his new recruits relieve himself by the fire, but it mattered not. He had enough men to achieve his goal.

Finally, the prince stopped in front of a man wearing a crimson shirt and torn brown leggings. His curly hair stood straight out in all directions.

"What's your name, sir?" the prince asked, thinking he looked rather familiar.

"Sir, my name is Roone." He jutted his chin out.

"Roone," he mused. "That's an interesting name.

Any chance you know Sir Antoine Roone?" His eyebrows lifted, but the man stood still, showing no signs of recognition. Antoine Roone, the infamous mercenary, was willing to do anything for the right price. His lack of scruples had earned him the nickname, 'The Monster of the Woods.'

"I do not know that name, sir."

"Just as well; he is a monster, after all." Prince Paulsen smiled as he saw the corners of Roone's mouth turn up at the insult, knowing he had the right man. "Either way, Roone, you're perfect for a special job I have in mind."

"Gentlemen, woodsmen, fighting men…" Prince Paulsen stopped to look around. Scanning the gathering crowd, he adjusted his thoughts. "On second thought, moneymen!" Everyone cheered.

"I am here to offer you what you have been dreaming of, what you have been looking for, what you have been killing for," he continued with a wink. "Too much has been withheld from us, and now it is time. We will take back what should be ours!" He thought of Madeline.

The snow began to fall through the trees.

"Men," he yelled, raising his sword, "Help me throw down the king and secure your wealth. Are you with me?"

The roar was so loud the forest animals ran deeper into the woods. The wind stopped blowing, as if the kingdom was holding its breath.

CHAPTER TEN

Madeline tossed in her sleep as the visions of fog became more and more clear. Her nose and eyebrows wrinkled as she felt the mist on her face. No fear plagued her as she walked through the soft white shadows. With each step, she moved deliberately towards a figure in green.

The figure stayed out of reach, beyond this tree, then behind another, giving Madeline a direction to follow, but no help. They danced around the trees for what seemed to be hours, until she found herself at the mouth of a dark cave.

Before she could react, she heard a soft whisper floating in the breeze. A gentle, soothing voice, singing in the wind, whispering her name. "Madeline, sweet Madeline. Come see. This is where you'll need to be."

Madeline glided forward. The dirt was soft and the air clammy and cool against her skin. Her heart beat faster and faster the closer she got to the cave. The bravery she had felt disappeared, and trepidation took its place. Closing her eyes, she took a deep breath and stepped into darkness.

"You must come here," the voice said, echoing off into the walls. "You must come here."

Princess Madeline startled awake, sweat beading

on her face, heart pounding. Wiping her arm over her forehead, she closed her eyes, trying to sort out what was real and what was a dream. It took her a moment to register that she had been moved back to her old room in the castle. The soft pink blankets were crumpled together at the foot of her bed, evidence of her restless night. She didn't use this room very often anymore, preferring the tower, but tonight, it was comforting.

Her head spun. A message from her mother, wizard powers, dragons—what had her mother known? And what was she getting herself into?

She needed to find answers. One thing was certain: she was not going to find them sleeping. She sat up and rolled out of bed.

The brisk air cooled her face as she made her way through the quiet corridors toward the library. Her slippered feet made soft taps on the stone floor. She turned the corner, surprised to see the candles burning already. Someone else had gotten the same idea. Curious, she crept to the door, peeking around the corner to see if she wanted the company or should go to her father's study instead.

She let out a sigh of relief when she saw the robed man hunched over the table. One hand traced the designs on his parchment; the other rubbed his temples. Feeling her eyes on him, Elias sat up and turned to look.

"Hello, Princess," he said with a smile, stopping his work and waving her in. "I'm glad you're up and feeling better."

"Yes, thank you," Madeline replied with a shy smile. She walked into the library. "Yesterday was an interesting day," she said, approaching the table. "What are you doing up at this time?" she asked, thinking of her own reasons for being up so early.

"This is the best time of day for me," Elias said. "Most people are still asleep, the sun is waiting to make its appearance, and the silence in the air is a welcome calm that helps get me through the chaos that comes later." He paused for a moment in reflection. "It gives me a moment to myself, to recharge, focus, and grow before the weight of the day."

Madeline sat down across from him at the table and rested her elbows on top. "So, tell me, when you made your choice, what was it like?"

Elias smiled and leaned forward with a whisper. "It was magic," he said. "For me, it was wonderful. It gave meaning and focus to my life that I had never felt before. It was as if that missing piece of me had been found and put into place. That feeling, that knowing that you're where you're supposed to be, doing what you're supposed to be doing..." he said in wonder. He looked at her, but her eyes were turned down, and she was biting her lower lip.

"Then, the hard work began," Elias said, gauging what she needed to hear. Madeline smiled. "Just as you learn from your tutors, wizards learn from our elders. We may have gifts, but they still must be trained and developed. The wizard training grounds here in the castle were below the grand hall, where the new dungeon is. Back then, they were filled with excitement, danger, exotic smells, and spices. It was a hall of learning, divining, and teaching. There was so much to study. There still is. Not a day goes by without a moment of learning and growth. Those are the cornerstones of a wizard's life—teaching, learning, and mystifying. Sometimes that last part is the most fun."

"Are we all wizards then? Those that choose that path?" she asked.

"No, not at all. That choice simply means that you accept the special gift. How far you choose to develop it depends on you. The gift could be divining, premonition, or something else; it all depends on what interests you, what natural skill stands out," Elias said, hoping to put her more at ease. "Since you are already past that initial stage, you might have already sensed something new."

Princess Madeline rested her head in her hands, thinking about her nightmares. "It seems like every day there is something new. It just feels like there is so much to learn, a whole new world that I didn't even know I was a part of. Like this," she pointed down at his parchments. "What does this mean?" she asked, pointing to a symbol on the maps in the shape of an arch. "I've seen them all over Professor Warren's maps, but he doesn't know what they mean. They look like the Dragon's Gate arch."

Elias looked down, "Oh yes," he said. "They have a special meaning. Those mark the gateways to magic and marvels."

Madeline looked at him with her own smirk. "Elias, please."

Elias grinned back. "Those are the markings of the openings of the ancient tunnels that were built for direct travel between regions. They were used by the wizards for communication with others without arousing suspicion." Elias reached over the table and held Madeline's hand in his. "Madeline, I would be honored to help instruct you and guide you. We'll make sense of it together."

Madeline looked at their hands and saw the love in his eyes. She nodded. "I would like that, Elias."

The sun peeked in through the window. Beautiful rays of crimson and orange shone down on the parchment.

"Time to welcome the day," he said, rising and collecting his papers.

CHAPTER ELEVEN

The air was frigid, a cold, blustery night that made their lips shrink and their arms press against their bodies for warmth. Snow slushed beneath their feet, and the winds howled defiantly, blasting them with chills as they continued through the woods, twigs crunching under their footsteps. They could see their breath, like steam out of a bull's nostrils before its attack. A ragtag bunch, they didn't march in any traditional formations or wear any customary armor. Nor were they united in their reasons for fighting. Some were pledged to uphold the honor of their prince, others came for money, and a few were simply out of their minds. Whatever their reasons, Prince Paulson used them to his advantage. With this last chance to acquire Princess Madeline, failure was not an option.

The morning sun continued to rise. They reached the outer edge of the forest and came upon the small community of thatched houses, stables, and farmland that surrounded the castle. Light trails of steam rose from the roofs as the warmth of the sun beat down. A handful of chimneys were smoking with morning fires, and the aroma of fresh bread filled the air. A dozen of the men were up early in the fields, organizing tools, hitching up horses, or making final preparations for the fall festival. They worked, oblivious to the growing mob at the forest's edge.

Prince Paulsen lined his men up, quieted their grunts, and regained their focus. "This is it, men, here is where we start: the king's village. They are nothing but poor workers, weak fighters, and fools. Let's show them what happens when they keep things that are not theirs. Take no prisoners and leave no spoils!"

The men grunted in response, lighting their torches and marching through the golden wheat fields towards the village.

The villagers had little time to react. Looking up from their work, they saw the mercenaries coming at them with raised torches. When a half-dozen mercenaries dropped their torches in the field, fire streamed through the air toward the villager's homes. Confusion gave way to fear as the first house went up in flames.

Screams rose through the air, and the men ran for weapons. The women and children fled towards the castle walls, babies wailing as their mothers threw them up on their shoulders and ran with all their might up the hill, not looking back in fear of the enemy's approach.

Prince Paulsen's men were thorough. They touched their torches to each home in the village, laughing as the roofs erupted in flames, the fire eagerly eating the homes and all the items within. Fights broke out over the gold and heirlooms that weren't destroyed by the fire. Metal clanged against metal. Prince Paulsen raised his sword.

"Men!" he yelled. "We do not stop here; this battle continues to the castle! Onward!" he shouted, kicking his horse.

Stomping to the front, he led his mercenaries out of the town. Smoke billowed up in their wake, showing their path of destruction to all.

Panic marred the faces of the crowd as King Theodore ordered the gates raised for his villagers to enter. He was astounded. Nothing like this had happened in the kingdom for decades. And now it happened on his watch. Each scream of pain felt like a stab wound in his stomach.

"Men!" King Theodore ordered, "this gate stays open until all villagers are in. See to their safety. I will see to the attackers." King Theodore twisted his body and stormed into the hall, calling for his knights and Prince Braden to meet him on the upper platforms.

Each step up the stairs fueled the king's anger. By the time he reached their vantage spot, his face matched the crimson of his robe. His eyes gazed over the surrounding area. It was clear what had happened. Plumes of smoke rose high into the sky, blackening the air. He heard the pained cries of his men, the fearful shrieks of the women, and the wailing of the children. Footsteps sounded on the stairs. Prince Braden and Daniel arrived at the top of the tower.

"Father, what's happening?" Braden asked, his eyes widening as he looked down at the village. "What did this?"

Daniel looked from side to side, his face hardening as he focused on the group coming toward them. "Your Majesty," he said, pointing to the mercenaries. "We have company."

"Who is it? Who has done this?" Braden demanded, peering as far as he could over the edge.

"Look closely at the man in front: his armor, that lion on his chest. That is our enemy." King Theodore replied.

"That can't be," Braden protested. "That's Prince Paulsen's crest."

"Yes, Paulsen is behind this. Now we must figure out why," King Theodore said, cupping his hand on Braden's shoulder.

At that moment, Princess Madeline, Sophia, and Elias joined the men on the platform. Madeline's brown hair flowed behind her in the wind. Her eyes glistened at the sight before her.

"Father," she said, horror in her voice. "What's going on here? The courtyard is full of our villagers, frightened for their lives."

Sophia peeked over the edge and covered her eyes to hide her growing tears.

"When the lion attacks the dragon, a new beginning awakens," Elias mused, recalling the cryptic words of the parchment.

Prince Paulsen's mercenaries had nearly reached the castle walls. Their sweaty stench rotted the air around them as they trampled their way forward. Their faces were muddy, fire-singed, and deranged by the time they approached the gates. Paulsen stood back and shook his hair in the wind. Looking up, he smiled as his eyes caught a glimpse of Princess Madeline on the tower above.

"Princess," he yelled so all could hear. "You will be mine! I am here for you!" He tossed his head back. At his command, his men started forward, banging their hands on the steel gates.

Princess Madeline shivered as her eyes connected with Paulsen's. She looked over at Daniel, her lips trembling.

"But I don't understand. Prince Paulsen? Why?" Madeline asked, remembering the man she had danced with at her betrothal ball. "He seemed so… so genuine. What happened?" Her voice shook, reeling at the sight before her.

"I know, my dear," said King Theodore, trying to console her. The rest looked on, uncertain of their next step. Daniel reached out to hold Madeline's hand in his.

Prince Braden and King Theodore looked at each other and then back to the others, shaking their heads.

"Badness isn't always easy to see, Madeline," said Prince Braden, "Sometimes it is simply felt in the heart. There has been something off about Paulsen ever since I first saw him come in looking for you.

When he came back, demanding you, it had grown worse. He felt entitled. Those feelings rarely add up to anything good, and now…" he trailed off, waving his hand, motioning to the countryside.

"Some shift in his character has created all this?" she asked, watching the chaos below. Their people ran inside the square, gathering supplies for easier storage and dispersal. "How can we shift him back? There has to be a solution."

"A solution to his character?" Prince Braden asked, "I fear it's too late for that. We need a plan of action."

"An answer to this attack," Daniel jumped in, offering his support. "Sometimes, Madeline," he said, "battle is simply a way to right a wrong when all other avenues are closed."

"And have all avenues been closed?" she demanded, tears in her eyes. "There has to be a way to stop this without more bloodshed."

"I don't know my dear," King Theodore said, "but we will try. Gentlemen, to my study."

"Father," Princess Madeline pleaded, "let me join."

"Some things are still for the men to decide," her father said. They walked out to make their battle plan.

Princess Madeline stared as the men disappeared into the tower stairs. Daniel glanced back with a saddened smile before following orders. Madeline's outrage subsided, and a half-smile grew in its place.

"They don't think they're going to get away with

it that easy, do they?" she asked, looking at Sophia. "It's a princess's duty to serve and protect her kingdom, right?"

"Oh no, Madeline," Sophia shook her head. "What are you thinking this time?"

Sophia shook her head. "What are you thinking?"

CHAPTER TWELVE

Princess Madeline grabbed Sophia's hand and pulled her toward the stairs.

"Madeline, stop, that hurts," Sophia said, pulling her arm back and rubbing the spot Madeline's fingers had grasped. "Where are we going?" Sophia looked at her friend.

Madeline took a deep breath. "Sophia, I don't know exactly what I'm going to do yet, but I need your help. The men can make their plans, but I can't just sit here and wait. Prince Paulsen attacked us because of me. This is all because of me." She grabbed Sophia's arm again. "I need to do something, but you have to trust me."

Sophia wavered, deliberating between her devotion to Prince Braden and her friendship with Madeline. "I will help you," she said, resigned, "but don't get hurt. You have to promise me."

Madeline smiled at her friend and raised her right hand in an oath. "Of course I'll stay safe. I promise." She gave her a quick hug and grabbed her arm again, leading her down to the library.

Madeline rushed around the room, grabbing maps, notes, and old war books. Sophia looked on as Madeline struggled to the table, her arms overloaded. They filled the library's few tables end-to-end with books, maps, and scrolls.

Their heads were down, focused on each of their books, when they heard a soft cough at the door. Madeline looked up and saw a boy about their age standing in the doorway. His green robe gave him away as one of Elias's group.

"I thought maybe I could help you," he said, his eyes fixed on the ground. "I saw you run down here from the castle walls. With so much going on, I thought I could help. I'm Emmett."

Madeline smiled and ran over to him, grabbing his arm and pulling him into the room. "Emmett, thank you," she said with a broad smile. "We need all the help we can get."

Madeline explained what they were looking for, and Emmett got to work. He sat at the table with Sophia and looked over the maps while she perused some old scrolls.

"I don't know what you're hoping to find," Sophia said after a while had passed.

Madeline sighed. "To tell you the truth, I don't know either. I thought something was going to jump out at me and tell me that this was what we needed to focus on."

"Do you know what you want to do?" Emmett asked. "If you know that, then we can go from there to make a plan."

"You make it sound simple," Madeline said, realizing that it should be. The simple plans always seemed to work best. She knew she'd get bogged down with too many details.

"We're looking for a battle plan," she said, thumbing through her own notes. Embarrassed, she showed Emmett and Sophia the pages from the day she had learned about Hawthorne's Theory. "Something like this."

Sophia smiled at the sketches Madeline had drawn of herself and Daniel, but Emmett went straight to the point. "That could work, Princess; something simple like this is perfect. We have no way to get out there though, to distract and surround them, without being noticed. We're inside, and they are right on the other side of the castle gates." His confidence grew as he spoke. He felt excited to have found a place to be and a way to help.

"We can if we do it this way," Madeline said, her voice picking up speed, her fingers flipping through papers until she found the map she was looking for. "Here, right here on the map," she said, pointing to an arch marked under the castle. "And here," she added, pointing to the other arch in the great forest.

Emmett smiled. "A tunnel is perfect."

Madeline looked at him in surprise. "You know what that symbol is?"

"We have lots of tunnels in the caves where I grew up. As an apprentice, I've been down them all. They say that the tunnels were once used as safe passage for wizards through all the territories, hidden underground. The tunnels to the north and south were collapsed by the dragons, and I guess these others haven't been used since the days of the exile. We need to find the opening. We can do this together." He grabbed the girls' hands.

Sophia looked down at Emmett's hand and grinned back at him tentatively. "Where do we begin?"

Madeline interrupted, "The dungeon. Let's go."

The three of them dashed through the hall until they reached the courtyard. People huddled in every corner, trying to find a place in the crowded square. Women cried, afraid to let their children down. The armed guards walked through on patrol, trying to keep order and calm. They held hands, afraid to lose one another in the crowd.

Inch by inch they made their way from one side of the courtyard to the other, trying to remain unnoticed. Emmett's face remained hidden beneath his hood, and Madeline and Sophia kept their heads down. Madeline looked around discreetly, feeling the anguish of her villagers as they struggled to find a place to sit, a place to weep. The snow settled on the cobblestones, chilling everyone to their bones. Their faces grimaced with pain. Madeline clenched her teeth, more determined than ever. These people were hurt because of her, and every one of their cries felt like a heavy weight added to her shoulders.

Madeline found the entrance to the dungeon and let out a sigh of relief: no guards. Looking left and right to make sure no one had seen them, she pulled as hard as she could and opened the door. The three of them slid inside as quickly as they could and closed the door behind them.

The air was cold and dusty, sending Sophia into a coughing fit. Madeline found it hard to imagine the magic that Elias had spoken about. The dungeon's rough walls were stained, the crevices home to colonies of mold. Piles of dirt and hay littered the floor. Emmett saw her scrunch her nose up at the smell, and chuckled.

"It was even worse inside the cells," he said, recalling his brief imprisonment. "Let's find the opening. I'm not sure it's the same, but in our caves, we have the arch marked on the wall, so even those wizards who cannot see can feel where it is."

Emmett started on one end of the room, Madeline and Sophia on the other. The walls were cold, but the dust and dirt did not bother them once they got started. Urgency spurred them on.

Madeline found it. Her fingers traced the outline of the carved arch above a locked wooden door.

"This must be the entrance," she said. "Now we need to find a way to open it."

Emmett gave her a wink. "At my princess's command." He reached into his robe and pulled out a wand and some powder.

Sophia watched him with a silly smile.

He closed his eyes and took a deep breath. Exhaling, he opened his eyes and focused on the lock. He pointed the wand, touching the tip to the steel, and blew the powder toward the end of his wand. The powder sizzled as the wand twisted the lock. Emmett bowed deeply to Princess Madeline. "Your Highness, here is your tunnel."

Princess Madeline let out a squeal of joy as she hugged Emmett and Sophia. She had a plan.

CHAPTER THIRTEEN

The grisly scene below worsened. The king's men watched, mouths slack and brows furrowed as insults and rocks were hurled at the castle walls. The men were tired. King Theodore's face had grown piqued and pale. Braden's temper burned as Prince Paulsen continued his tirade below.

The growls echoing from the ground sounded like a slaughterhouse. Their beautiful sky had been blackened with smoke, and the harmonious sounds that usually filled the air were exchanged for the yells of a raucous mob.

It was the second day of the siege, and no progress had been made on either side. Prince Paulsen seemed content to stand his ground outside the walls, mocking and harassing the guards above as he paced.

On top of the platforms, King Theodore's men kept watch. Daniel led the knights, yelling out orders and maintaining their defense. His face was tight, his lips pursed, refusing to give any hint of weakness to Prince Paulsen and his men. But he knew it couldn't last forever. His legs were tired from running the length of the castle walls, his throat sore from calling out new orders.

The wind blew against his hair and face, clearing his mind. There was no time to focus on his worry. It was his time to act, to protect his kingdom and princess.

King Theodore and Prince Braden looked back and forth between the inner courtyard and the mercenaries outside, discussing their options as Daniel approached from the west corner. "Your Majesty, Your Highness," he said, pointing to the commotion below. "The area is protected. I have surveyed every corner, and there are no evident weaknesses. The castle walls are high and strong, and the men are brave and ready. Most of the villagers have been accounted for and are settled into new dwellings for the time being. Supplies are still being counted and divided up for rationing. We can hold this position for as long as we need to, or we can move on your command at any time." Daniel's steel gray eyes were steady and sure.

King Theodore's robe billowed in the wind as strategies formed in his mind. Glancing down, he could literally see both sides of the problem. On one side of the wall, Prince Paulsen and his men pounded on the gate, swords drawn, faces scowling. On the other side sat the villagers, heartbroken and wounded, huddled together for warmth and comfort as they relived the destruction of their homes. The wind and snow continued to gather as the king rubbed his beard, hoping their strategy was right.

With a quick glance at Braden and Elias, King Theodore cleared his throat and spoke loudly and clearly.

"At this moment, we stay, we stand tall and strong. Our fortress is secure, our men's vision clear. Winter is setting in, and we're on the better footing. Let the snow freeze them and their tempers. Our people have seen enough tragedy for now." His eyes swept over the horizon, filling with tears at the memories of the carnage.

Prince Braden nodded in agreement, clasping his hands on the castle walls. "I agree, Father," he said, looking down at Paulsen. "It's the best plan for now." Daniel looked them both in the eyes and nodded before returning to his men.

Sophia grabbed the soft velvet lining of Madeline's dress. The princess dropped the bag she had hastily packed for the trip.

"Madeline, please," Sophia begged. "You can't just leave. You have to tell your father, and consider all your options."

Madeline stopped for a second and turned to face her friend. Holding Sophia's hands in hers, she offered a sad smile. "I understand you're scared. I am too, but we don't have time to think about that right now. Our village is gone, destroyed right before the festival. Our people are displaced, our harvest and food scattered, land taken siege, and why? All for Prince Paulsen's obsession with me."

Her eyes searched Sophia's face and saw it soften. "It's my duty as princess, but also as a person, to try to find a solution for this. I have to try,"

Madeline said firmly.

Sophia knew her friend's mind was set, and she also suspected she was right. "It is your duty to be prepared, but it is also your duty to be safe," she said. "That means talking to your father first. Try to get his help." Sophia let her hands go, satisfied with her lecture, and grabbed something from behind her. "You'll need this," she said, handing her a hooded blue woolen cape. They exchanged a quick smile before Madeline finished packing. She wouldn't be gone long, but she still wanted to be prepared.

With Sophia's help, Madeline changed into a soft white dress with leather trim. It was made for movement, fitting closely where it needed to. Sophia pulled Madeline's hair back away from her face in a loose braid, functional but still beautiful. Before she left, she slipped on her shell necklace. Daniel had found the green shell on his adventure last summer while searching for her. She wore it close to her heart. Its soft, reflective rainbows sparkled around the room. At the very least, she would look every inch a princess.

Madeline smiled as she saw herself evolve in the mirror, feeling her friend's support. "Thank you," Madeline said. "It's time to go." She reached around to squeeze her friend's hand.

"Yes, but first," Sophia said, "go see your father."

Madeline's heart sank. "My father?" she asked,

dreading the answer. "I thought you understood why I am doing this."

"If you want my help, then you need to at least try to show that you have learned from last summer. I understand, but I'm not going to let you be reckless. You can't leave while we're under siege."

"I'll be back before he notices," Madeline protested, knowing even as she said it that her friend was right.

"What happens if, for some reason, you aren't?" Sophia asked, concern in her eyes. "I'm helping you, but I'm not convinced that this is going to work. What happens to your father, or to Daniel, if you're captured? Please, talk to him. Try," she pleaded. "Show him how much you've grown."

Resigned, Madeline nodded in agreement.

"Absolutely not," King Theodore yelled, his face turning as red as the sunset in the background. "I don't know what has gotten into your head, Madeline. We're waiting this out. Prince Paulsen will be gone before you know it."

"What if he's not? What if he holds out for the winter? What happens to our storage of food or to the villagers camped in the main square?" Madeline demanded, pointing down at the scattered people. "He has already ruined our fall festival; don't let him ruin our lives. Yes, I'm sure we can survive this way for a while, but is there another option? I think there is, if you just let me try," she implored.

King Theodore shook his head. "My dear daughter, you speak with your heart, and I applaud you for trying to find a solution. But this matter is settled."

"Shouldn't we be answering his demands? Shouldn't we put a stop to all this madness?"

"We will, daughter, in due time. Right now, we give time for the snow to freeze him out. What you're suggesting is too dangerous."

King Theodore gave Madeline a tight-lipped, definitive smile and walked away.

She muttered under her breath, "I tried, Father, I really did. The risk of doing nothing is higher than you think, and I can't allow that." The wind blowing through her hair, the chill of the snow cooling her skin, and the howls from Prince Paulsen's men below made her answer clear. She was going to put a stop to this.

Focused on her destination, she didn't see Daniel until she turned the corner. "Madeline," he said gently, reaching out to touch her arm.

"Oh, Daniel," she said falling into his arms, seeking his comfort and warmth. "What's going on here?" she asked.

"I don't know, Madeline, I don't know. But you are safe. He can't hurt you," Daniel said, his voice strong and sure.

"Daniel," Madeline started, "I have a plan."

"Don't worry, Madeline, we have it taken care of. There's nothing to worry about."

"I do worry, though," she said softly.

"We'll get through this together," Daniel assured her with a smile. "No one is taking you from me." He lifted her chin into a kiss.

The sun went down over the kingdom. Madeline and Daniel stood arm in arm, watching the blood-red horizon turn dark.

A couple of hours later, as the men continued to stand guard on the castle walls, Princess Madeline hesitated at the opening of the tunnel in the catacombs. Dressed in her wool cape, with her bag on her shoulder, she took a deep breath and pushed the tunnel door open.

"Wait," a deep voice whispered behind her.

Madeline's heart fluttered, her breath stuck in her throat.

"You aren't going anywhere," the voice said.

Madeline whirled around. Emmett and his brothers stood in the shadows. "You can't go without us," he said with a shy smile.

She breathed out a sigh of relief. "Are you ready for this?" she asked.

"No," he said, shrugging, "but who is?"

She felt some of the weight lifting off her shoulders. "Let's go," she said, pushing the door open and taking the first step into darkness.

CHAPTER FOURTEEN

The tunnels had not been used since before the exile, and sixteen years of disuse had not been kind to them. The air was cold and musty, and the rancid smell made Madeline's stomach tighten up. She ducked to avoid a dusty cobweb and nearly tripped over a broken cobblestone. It wasn't an inviting path, but she knew they needed to take it.

They moved quietly, as if breaking the silence might shatter the magic. Madeline's thoughts raced back and forth between her visions of Prince Paulsen leering up at her, the women and children 'left cold and homeless in the castle square, and the dark vastness before her.

The cobblestones only lasted for a short distance in the tunnel. Soon, the pathway turned into a rocky floor, littered with large boulders and haunted by dark shadows that seemed to reach out at her. Her heart beat a little faster. She had never been enclosed like this before and didn't like it. Not at all. The weight of the tunnel seemed to constrict her throat.

Sparing a quick glace around her, Madeline took courage. She had not anticipated having company, but Emmett and his brothers proved to be helpful companions, moving rocks that had fallen into the main path, carrying the torches to light their way, and cheering her up with the jovial spirit that they exuded.

Her heart kept pace with her toes: the further they stepped, the faster it pounded. She walked on the balls of her feet, leaving the smallest of footprints, almost as if to hide their tracks.

What was she doing? Worry snuck into her mind. She was a princess. Never before had she been to battle, let alone tried to devise a strategy. What if she was endangering herself or her friends needlessly? She bit her lower lips as she stole a glance at the men helping guide her through the tunnel. She pushed the thoughts to the side and wiped the hair and sweat from her face.

There was no room for those thoughts now. The four of them were on the move, and if she stopped to think about it, she might turn around and return to her father. She felt in the pit of her stomach that this was the right path. It was time to move forward.

As they rounded the next corner, their feet stopped in their tracks. Princess Madeline lifted her hand to her chest, taking a deep breath as something clicked into place. The brothers stood to the side, mouths agape.

"Emmett," Princess Madeline squealed. "Look at this, all around!" She twirled in awe, looking at all the openings before them. They had entered what seemed to be the main chamber, a circular room with at least ten entrances evenly spaced along the edge of the room. The cobblestones that made up the floor were arranged in a circular pattern around the room, spiraling in toward the center. The walls were smooth, and there were marble markers outside each opening.

Princess Madeline ran to an entrance and stroked her fingertips on the smooth face of one of the placards. All at once the dust disappeared, and the sheen of the marble sparkled in the torchlight. Magic filled the air, waiting to be enchanted again.

Emmett pointed to the placard in front of him. "This one looks like a tree, Princess, come look!" He waved her over with his arms. His brothers dashed from doorway to doorway, awakening each slab of marble with their touch.

"This must take us further into the forest," Princess Madeline said. She ran to the next, "Look! This one has an arch; it must be the path to Dragons Gate. And here, the symbol for water. This must go down south to the bay! We've found them!"

"Which one do we take?" asked one of Emmett's brothers.

"Follow me!" She lifted the hem of her dress and took off down the path marked by the tree.

The brothers could barely keep up as Madeline ran ahead, her heart now pumping more with anticipation than fear.

They wandered down the new tunnel for hours until they noticed the path around them starting to get lighter. They were approaching the end of the tunnel and saw the forest in the early morning light.

Princess Madeline approached the edge of the tunnel cautiously, listening for any noises as she peeked outside its rocky edge. The cool breeze blew against her face, bringing the sweet smell of pine and fresh dirt and lifting her hair. Her stomach tightened. They were here.

"Princess," Emmett said, breaking her thoughts. "What now?" His hands and face were covered in dirt and soot. His attempts to wipe them only smeared the grime into his robes.

Princess Madeline looked from him to his brothers and took a deep breath. "Wait here," she said, smoothing out her dress as she stepped forward. The linen dress was now more brown than white, and her braid had fallen out some time ago, leaving her hair cascading in loose waves down her back. Her cheeks were smudged with dirt. But in spite of the journey, she stood with her back straight and tall. Emmett thought she looked more like a princess than she ever had before.

Her mind turned with each step she took. Each tree she passed seemed a bit more familiar, each rock more recognizable. A tingling sensation grew in the pit of her stomach, a nagging thought that she had been here before, a whispered memory of dancing around these trees. Looking back over her shoulder, she half-expected to see someone watching her.

As she turned around, her eyes focused on the opening to the tunnel. From this angle, it looked exactly like the cave from her dream. She *had* been here before, and she was exactly where she needed to be.

CHAPTER FIFTEEN

The sun rose slowly on the third day of battle, as if it dreaded what it would see. Prince Paulsen's men stood at the base of the castle walls, unable to break their defenses. The king's knights were in full-scale defensive mode, alternating groups to stand guard day and night. Daniel watched Prince Paulsen's every move. Their weary eyes met often, their gazes waging their own battle of dedication and desperation.

Prince Paulsen was unnerved. As a prince and soldier, he was mentally prepared for the long haul. His soldiers were also aware that sieges could take time. His new recruits, however, were losing their focus. They wanted their reward now. The grumbles that they were still there became more prominent as their beards froze and their toes turned blue.

"Sir," Prince Paulsen heard from behind him. He turned to see the forest man, Roone. "You called for me?" the mercenary asked, one hand on his sword hilt.

"Yes, yes, thank you for coming so quickly," Prince Paulsen said. "It seems some of the men are growing restless. It's time to put our plan into action. This is a special assignment, specifically chosen for a man of your skills and temperament. Do you think you're up for it?" he asked, tilting his head.

"Yes sir," Roone replied, standing taller.

Prince Paulsen nodded. "Good, good." He patted him on the back and handed him a letter. "You'll deliver this to the messengers at the gate and then return to the far side of the castle and wait. Beyond that ridge is a small grouping of trees that will make an excellent hiding spot. Wait there until you hear my call. They'll never know what happened," his laughter rang out as he clasped arms with Roone and handed over the message with his seal.

The king's messengers raced into the main hall, their armor clanking as they knelt before the throne. King Theodore jerked his head up, surprised at their sudden appearance.

"What is it, my good knights?" he asked. His arms gripped onto the edges of his throne.

A knight stepped forward. "Your Majesty, we received this at the gates this morning. It was delivered by one of Prince Paulsen's men." He brought the message forward and knelt.

"Let's see what we have here," King Theodore said, reading through the note. His face turned red as he shook it in the air. "This is outrageous!" He clenched his teeth. "Braden, read this," he said, tossing the message toward him. "Guards, bring in Sir Daniel. He is being requested."

The guards hurried out as fast as they came in.

Nervous tension filled the hall as Prince Braden looked over the message. King Theodore continued to mutter under his breath, rubbing his hands together, frustration evident in the furrows of his brow.

"Father," Prince Braden said, finishing the message and handing it back to the king. "What does this mean? What is his plan?"

"This," the king said, "is the request of a madman." His face shook as the grand doors opened and Daniel approached.

Daniel's face was flushed, his skin smeared with dirt, sweat, and grease, and his hair slicked back. His eyes were red and weary but still focused as he knelt before the king and prince, his helmet in one hand and the hilt of his sword in the other.

"Your Majesty, Your Highness," he said, approaching the throne. "Is there news?"

"Sir Daniel, you are always prepared to take action. Your position as Knight Champion shows your valor and strength, and I am proud that you have been chosen to protect Princess Madeline for life." King Theodore stepped down from his throne and approached him where he knelt.

"It seems, Sir Knight, that someone else wishes to take your position." King Theodore dropped his arm and held the papers out to him. "Prince Paulsen is requesting a man-to-man contest to end this stand-off."

"A man-to-man contest?" Daniel asked, looking over the letter. "Is this our next step?"

"Yes," said the king, letting out a deep sigh. "I

think this has to be, for the sake of the villagers. I think we must resolve this quickly."

"As Your Majesty requests," Daniel said, bowing his head deeply. "I'm ready."

The courtyard was silent in reverence for Daniel as he put on the remainder of his armor. His fellow knights patted him on the back and crossed their swords with his in a gesture of luck and goodwill. The women in the square crossed their hearts and blew him kisses to send him off with strength. Some of the children hid while others, out playing with their wooden swords, stopped to watch Daniel pass.

The steel gates creaked as they opened to the outside. The quiet reverence quickly gave way to raucous mocking.

Prince Paulsen's men had been moved back according to battle etiquette and were barricaded on the edge of the village. Prince Paulsen stood directly in front of Daniel, his sword dangling in one arm, leaning on the edge of his shield. He looked Daniel up and down, trying to find weakness, a fault he could prey upon. Sir Daniel stood tall, strong and firm, knowing that he was ready.

"You called for this contest," Daniel said, his voice clear and powerful.

"That I have, Sir Knight. You stole the prize the king promised to me, and now, to get it back, I must take care of you." Paulsen pointed his sword at Daniel.

"Princess Madeline is not a prize, Prince Paulsen. She is our princess, the jewel of our kingdom, and a woman to be respected," Daniel said firmly. Raising his arms, sword drawn and shield in position, Daniel clenched his jaw and set his feet, prepared for Paulsen's attack.

The top platforms filled quickly as the crowd ran to get a better view of the battle. King Theodore, Prince Braden, Elias, and the knights stood in the front, watching the events unfold below. Prince Braden gripped the edge of the stones, fingers sore from clutching so tight. King Theodore stood back, watching stiffly, knowing it should be himself engaged with Paulsen below. Elias stood by the king's left side, closing his eyes as the wind blew through the air, feeling the movement in the shifting air patterns.

"Now we wait, we watch, and we wish, Your Majesty," Elias said, keeping his eyes focused. "We watch," he repeated to himself, "as the lion attacks the dragon."

Daniel and Prince Paulsen's arms swung hard and fast, metal banging on metal as their swords dancing off the edge of each other's shields. Daniel pounded Paulsen hard: thrust after thrust, bouncing off, attacking, and engaging. Paulsen counter-attacked, pared off rocks, and pushed back. They seemed to be evenly matched, sword thrust for thrust.

After what seemed like hours of fighting,

Paulsen's foot slipped through the muddy snow, and he fell hard onto his back, snow and mud splashing out from underneath him. His head bounced off the ground, his shield swung off just out of reach. A chill crawled down Daniel's spine as Paulsen's helmet fell off, revealing crazed madness in his eyes.

Daniel reached his arms up to the sky and braced for the final strike, hesitating. Paulsen rotated his sword horizontally and blocked the downward strike. Daniel gritted his teeth and leaned forward, pushing with all the intensity he could muster. Paulsen spat up in his face and hurled insults between breaths as the sword slid closer and closer to his throat. The metallic reverberation filled the air around them as the swords connected. His mouth soured with the sweat dripping from Daniel's cheeks.

Pure and utter madness sounded in the air as Paulsen began to laugh shrilly. "You made one fatal mistake, Daniel," Prince Paulsen said, sneering at him, holding his sword in two hands and pressing back up at Daniel.

"What's that?" Daniel asked, pushing harder.

"You thought that I would play fair," he said. Prince Paulsen threw his head back and yelled into the air. A madman appeared from beyond the bushes, wild-eyed and ready to attack.

Daniel looked over his shoulder just in time to see a massive warrior running toward him with his sword drawn overhead.

Daniel jumped back, allowing Paulsen to

scramble to his feet and reposition his sword. Now the two men stood in front of Daniel, their swords dancing from hand to hand as Daniel looked on with new fear entering his eyes.

Prince Braden jumped up, eyes bulging as he saw the man running in from outside. "Father," he yelled, "look at what's happening!"

"This is an outrage," King Theodore sputtered, his nostrils flaring, hands gripping the tower walls. "He is defying every rule of battle protocol. Braden," he said, pointing to the rest of the knights. "Get out there and protect Daniel. Let's end this battle now!"

Elias raised his arms and pointed out over the field. His eyes still focused on the battlefield. "Your Majesty, wait," he demanded, motioning to the far edges of the field. "Paulsen's men seem to be heading back to the forest. Why are they leaving when they have now taken the lead?"

King Theodore turned back and looked over his shoulder to the field where Elias pointed.

"Men, wait!" King Theodore said. "Something is happening." He gazed into the distance. Turning, he looked Elias and Prince Braden straight in the eyes, frustrated that he didn't know the answer. None of them knew.

CHAPTER SIXTEEN

Madeline stared hard at the tunnel opening. "Yes," she thought to herself, feeling a wave of relief and confidence roll over her. "This is where I am supposed to be, just as I saw. Now, if I only knew exactly how I was supposed to do this."

She paused for a moment, letting the cool breeze brush the wisps of hair out of her face. The cool temperature cleared her mind and allowed her to focus for a moment. Her eyes shifted up. She gazed over the trees, their soft and vibrant greens filling her mind with peace, the soft chirps of birds easing the knot of fear in her stomach. Even the dirt offered her comfort, the aroma of a fresh morning, pine needles and morning dew, the sweet smell of life. It was a vast difference from the musty containment of the tunnels, and a huge departure from the smoky destruction of her village.

She had to move. In theory, she knew what she was there to do. It had already been laid out. According to Hawthorne's Theory, she had to draw the men toward her so that they would surround her, and then the king's men could surround them in surprise and attack. The plan's simplicity did not calm the pounding of her heart.

Madeline lifted her eyes and looked straight at Emmett and his brothers. "Emmett," she said softly, trying to keep her voice as quiet as the whispers of wind. "I need you and your brothers to help me."

Emmett's eyes lit up at the request. He lifted his dusty hand to his brow and bowed forward theatrically. "Anything our princess requests."

His brothers stared at him, fear in their eyes. Their strong arms gripped the hilts of their swords, and their faces were set firmly. They nodded in agreement.

Madeline tried to contain her excitement. Despite the fear and dread she felt creeping up and tightening in her stomach, a calm awareness grew in her heart. Each pound of her heart was like a drum, guiding her forward to the next movement.

Grabbing a stick from the ground, she drew a quick formula in the freshly scuffed dirt. Sweeping circles and crosses depicted their movements. The brother's eyes opened wide as they looked from her, to the ground, and back to her.

"This could work, Princess," Emmett said, clapping his hands together. "This could work." He looked around to where they needed to be and quickly spoke to his brothers.

Madeline looked up around her and saw the morning sun reaching through the canopy above, stretching its rays to the ground, warming them with each stretch of its arm.

The group made their way slowly away from the tunnel entrance, careful to remember its exact location. Everything had to go according to plan.

They moved stealthily, quiet as deer in the forest.

Finding Paulsen's men was easier than they had expected. These were rough men, and their path through the forest had been trampled carelessly. A worn path used by the deer and elk had been widened to at least ten feet. The bushes stomped, the flowers trodden down—everything they passed by bore the mark of the mercenaries.

The air grew louder. Strange grunts followed cruel laughter. The birds became silent, the sky seemed to loom darker from the smoke, and the air took on the pungent smell of unclean bodies, blood, and grime. They were almost there.

With a quick nod from Princess Madeline, Emmett and his brothers climbed the nearest tree and waited. They took quick looks around them and marked their paths.

The fear and apprehension that had disappeared as they were walking came back threefold. Her face felt cold, her fingertips tingled, and her stomach was so tense she felt paralyzed for a moment. Taking deep breaths, she stepped forward, slowly, then stronger, getting into position and looking up for the signal. It took a moment to find the three brothers in the trees. They had found a way to blend in, their dirt-stained pants blending into the branches, and their green robes hiding them in the leaves.

Emmett leaned down and covered his mouth with his hands, whistling like a bird to signal they were in place and ready. Madeline drew a quick circle on the ground with her toes to mark the location and lifted her head high. The wind blew, and she felt the strength inside her rise.

"Prince Paulsen," she cried into the air. "Prince Paulsen, I have heard your demands, and I am here. Let's stop this war and let all be. I am here now."

The wind rustled, the ground shook, but no one came. Taking a deep breath, easing the worry that they might not hear her, she refocused, planting her feet solidly into the ground.

"Prince Paulsen, you have demanded me, and here I am. I now demand that you come to me." Her hands balled together in fists by her side, her heart beating madly as she stood with a tense knot gnawing in her stomach.

The men crept out of the forest. Dark greens, blues, reds, and shiny silver and copper reflected off their swords as they came in closer. The air grew fouler the nearer they got, like rotten meat walking toward her.

Her nose wrinkled, her palms felt sweaty, and the knot in her stomach grew tighter. Her plan was working, but she knew that this was not going to be an easy trip. Her life, as well as the lives of Emmett and his brothers, was on the line. She also knew that bravery meant doing things when you didn't want to, even when you were scared. Her head turned, looking at each man in turn. Their snarls glared back at her. She searched for Prince Paulsen. His men surrounded her, but he was nowhere to be seen.

"I demand to see Prince Paulsen," she said in her loudest, most commanding voice, her head held high.

"He's not here, Princess. You'll have to deal with me instead," the closest man chuckled, showing crooked, brown teeth. His body was large and strong, and muscles bulged though the holes in his leggings and sleeves.

Princess Madeline held up her palm to stop him and looked him in the eyes. "I am here for Paulsen. And he will punish any one of you who comes near me. Whether you like it or not, it is him I will deal with, and only him. Bring him to me," she said, forcing her eyes to project a solid wall of enforcement. "Bring him here, now!" she demanded in a way she had heard her father talk to subjects.

The man stopped in his tracks and murmured to the others. They shook their heads, none of them moving closer and none of them moving to get Paulsen.

"He is busy at the moment, Princess, but we will keep you company until he can arrive. He is taking care of your knight as we speak." His laughter rang through the air. Daniel! She hadn't even thought about what was going on at the castle.

She kept her head high, trying to hide the tears starting to well up in her eyes and the worry growing in her belly. She had to wait until she knew the plan was going to work. This was still only the first phase. Until the signal sounded, she needed to keep the men from leaving. Her chest burned from taking deep breaths, especially now that the air was filled with their stench. It was the only way to keep her focus, to keep her still while she waited.

Sophia had been up all night, her mind counting the minutes, her thoughts going to dark places with fear over what could be happening. She had agreed to help Madeline, knowing it was the right thing to do, but not fully understanding how to play her part in the plan. The worry, the pacing, and the anticipation were all new feelings to her. They left her stomach torn and tumbled in knots. It had finally come time for her to take action.

With a deep breath, she looked up the stairs to the castle walls and tightened her lips together. How was she going to explain this to Braden and King Theodore? She lifted the bottom of her red gown and started to climb, hoping to find the right words. The tower walls loomed closer, but still, no plan entered her mind. Walking out onto the walls, she stopped, fear freezing her in place.

The king and Braden were pointing at the horizon. Men were clamoring all around, trying to see what was going on and where they needed to be. The air was thick with tension, sweaty armor, and smoke.

Her steps were slow and timid as she made her way toward the men, their voices hard with anger. Her stomach churned as she got closer, feeling lightheaded and nauseated with each step.

"Prince Braden," she said softly, touching him on

his elbow. He did not feel her. She bowed her head and took a deep breath. "Prince Braden, King Theodore," she said more loudly, clearing her throat. Her cheeks warmed when they stopped talking to look at her.

"Sophia," Braden said, surprised to see her. "What are you doing here?" he asked. "You're supposed to stay inside for safety."

"I, I..." she stammered, trying to find the right words.

"We are in the middle of a battle," he said, pointing to the field where Daniel was battling the two men.

"It's your sister."

"Madeline?" the king asked, his ears perking up. "What has she gotten herself involved in this time?" He crossed his arms, eyes boring into her.

Sophia cast her eyes downward, feeling the panic rise in her stomach as her face paled. "She is gone, Your Majesty."

"Gone?" he said incredulously.

"Sophia, what do you mean?" Prince Braden asked, grabbing her hands and forcing her to look up at him.

Fresh tears spilled down her cheeks as the worry she'd felt all night rushed to the surface. "Oh Braden," she said, looking up at him pleadingly, "she said she had to go, that there was no other way, it was her duty."

Prince Braden let her hands go, bewilderment in

his eyes. His face tightened. "Where did she go?" he demanded.

"She found the ancient tunnels that lead out to the woods," she said, pointing out onto the battlefield. "She said she had a plan, the only plan that could end this quickly without much destruction. She was determined. I had to help her."

"She already told me her plan," King Theodore fumed, "but I told her it was too risky. Hawthorne's Theory! Why does she have to be so stubborn?"

"Hawthorne's Theory?" Braden's eyes widened. "She's set herself up as bait. And if she's in the woods, Paulson's men are heading straight toward her." He paused for a moment. "We have no choice. We must attack now so she has a chance to escape. Oh, I wish she knew what she was doing," Prince Braden said, his eyes focused ahead, his jaw set in stone. "Sophia," he turned to her, betrayal and hurt echoing from his eyes. "How you could be involved in this? Why didn't you trust me?"

He looked away from her and turned to his father. Sophia dropped her eyes to the ground. No one saw her tears fall as she backed away slowly, slipping down the staircase.

"Men," King Theodore blared. "It is time for action. You there," he pointed to several men, "secure the castle and help Daniel against Paulsen; the rest of us need to protect our princess. She is out in the forest creating a diversion so we can divide and conquer."

Surprised murmuring ran through the air as the men looked at the king and the battlefield, their armor clanging as they shifted anxiously side to side.

"Get to your horses, men, and we ride. We will protect the princess and show these wildlings that they dare not attack the Kingdom of Soron! Are you with me?" the king roared to a deafening cheer.

Men raced down the stairs, passing Sophia without notice. She pressed her body in as close as she could to the wall, the pounding of their armor on the stairs drowning out her sobs. After the men had rushed by, Sophia composed herself and gathered her skirt to start down again.

"Wait, please," she heard behind her.

Turning, she saw Elias standing with his arm stretched out toward her. She walked up to him and took his hand as he pulled her into a soft hug.

"My dear," he said soothingly, "what you did was brave. Helping Madeline, helping the kingdom, putting yourself on the line..."

"But he hates me now," she whispered, the tears starting to fall again.

"How he feels may change or it may not, but it does not change the fact that you did what you needed to do. Being brave doesn't mean telling people what they want to hear. Being brave means doing the right thing in spite of how people may see you or react. Remember that," Elias said with a gentle pat. They walked back to the tower walls to oversee the action.

The king and his knights galloped past to save the princess as Daniel continued fighting off Roone and Paulsen. Roone was a large man, with wild hair and bulging arms. His face snarled into a manic grin, and his jaw jutted down like a bull ready to attack. His eyes were wild and red, looking around, unwilling to settle onto one place. Prince Paulsen seemed to relax a bit, feeling surer of himself, assuming the two of them would have no problem overpowering Daniel. Paulsen, now standing on two feet, gripped his sword firmly with one hand, while the other swept his hair back.

Daniel stared at the two of them, more focused than ever. Breathing deep to regain composure and energy, he dug his feet into the snow- and mud-filled field, lowering his body into battle stance. A sense of calm surrounded him. The fields grew quieter, the air softer, and the smells less distinct. The more he focused in on them, the less he noticed the surrounding area.

Paulsen jumped first, their metal swords bouncing off each other. Daniel easily blocked his jabs and pushed him off with his feet. Paulsen stumbled over a rock and found himself on his back again. Snow and mud sprayed up over his head.

Roone threw his head back in laughter and started forward, his arms raised high, ready to attack. He ran toward Daniel, kicking up mud and splashing it onto Paulsen's head. They connected, forcing

Daniel to his knees in a defensive move, his arms paring off the sword to the side. Roone was stronger than he looked, and he was thickly muscled. It was a struggle for Daniel to keep him off, aware that Paulsen was also climbing to his feet.

Daniel had to get one of the men down. Sparing quick glances around him, he noticed a small grove of trees to the right. If he could maneuver them there, he might have a chance.

He turned backward hoping to lead Roone astray. Roone followed. His laughter rang out as Daniel inched back, step by step toward the grove of trees. Daniel swung his sword. Sweat poured down his face, the drops itching as they mixed with the mud and dirt. Beat after beat, step after step, Daniel counted and fought. He saw the first small bush get trampled under Roone's muddy boots, the leaves hidden in the mud and snow.

Daniel knew he was in the right area. He recalled the location of the large roots, only a few steps away. One step back, two steps back, three steps. Daniel lifted his sword. With a great leap forward, he lunged at Roone, twisting to the side at the last moment. Roone leaned in to counter the attack and tripped over the outstretched branches. Daniel stood over him and smacked the hilt of his sword down on the mercenary's head. Roone slumped forward from the impact, passed out.

With one down, Daniel turned to see that Paulsen had regained his position and was running towards him.

Daniel took a deep breath and refocused. A small smile grew on his face as his confidence and rhythm resurfaced.

Paulsen saw Roone lying face down in the snow and slowed his steps. Looking back over his shoulder, he searched for an escape route. Daniel was too quick. Running faster and faster, he lunged toward him, yelling in anger and victory as his sword connected with all his strength. Their blades crashed. Snow crushed to the side, their boots sloshing in the mud. Fear rose in Paulsen's eyes as Daniel's focused on him with a new intensity.

Paulsen cowered under the weight of the sword, lifting his shield to block the blows, one after another. Daniel smiled as Paulsen curled into a ball under his shield, like a turtle hiding in the confines of his shell. Daniel stood triumphantly above him and hammered the sword down onto the shield one last time, knocking Paulsen out.

Exhilaration quickly turned to exhaustion as Daniel sat down next to Paulsen. Roone still lay motionless in the distance. Daniel leaned over, his helmet off in the mud somewhere as sweat dripped down his face and off his cheeks. His hair slicked back as he ran his fingers through it, showing his weary face and tired eyes. Tilting his head back, he could see the men and women cheering from the castle walls. Their arms waved wildly and their cheers rung out through the air.

CHAPTER SEVENTEEN

She heard a slight ringing in the air, a slow rumbling on the ground—the charge of the horses as her men drew near. It was time. Before she knew it, the soft charge became a full-blown thunder of activity.

The dragon banners of Soron raced through the air, dancing between the trees and sky. The horses snorted as they bolted through the woods, weaving in and out of trees, over rocks, and through brush on a mission to save their princess. The king's men came quickly, and before they knew what was happening, Prince Paulsen's men were surrounded. Their faces contorted into strange grins as they prepared for battle. They stood defensively with their hands on their swords, their feet planted in the ground, and their voices set in grunts and war whoops, ready to attack.

Once Princess Madeline saw the approach, she knew her time was limited. She needed to get out before someone grabbed her. Throwing her head back, she gave a quick whistle. Emmett and his brothers swung down from the trees to grab her. Before the woodsmen even knew what was happening, Madeline was gone, disappeared before their eyes. In another moment, they were surrounded by King Theodore's knights.

Out of breath, her chest heaving, Madeline looked at the three wizards and smiled. From ear to ear, all four of them shared the same grin, fighting hard to hold back their excitement. They were high up in the trees and had to make it back to the tunnel before they were found out.

Emmett led them back in the treetops, careful to show Madeline how to balance her feet over the branches for support. They needed to move through several hundred feet of tree canopy before they could drop down and run on the ground, certain that they were beyond all the fighting men and could travel safely.

Bit by bit, slower than Madeline thought possible, they walked through the treetops, hoping to remain unseen. Carefully placing the arch of her feet on the slender branches, Madeline moved at a snail's pace, feeling the sway of the tree throughout her body. Risking a few quick peeks at the fight, she saw bright flashes of swords and armor. She listened intently to the pace of the clanging metal, feeling her heartbeat quicken with intensity. The snorting horses, the smell of sweat, and the shrieks as woodsmen fell reassured her the battle was going well as she made her way forward. Each step lightened the weight on Princess Madeline's heart.

As soon as the battle sounds grew faint, the brothers carefully lowered Madeline down to the ground in the same fashion they picked her up. She smiled as they flipped down, as if they had done this sort of thing thousands of times. Emmett gave her a knowing wink.

Wasting no time, they ran as quickly as they could, jumping over rocks and dancing around trees, branches whipping their faces as they ran until familiar sights jumped out at them. A special rock here, a twisted tree there, the drawings in the dirt, they were back on the path to the tunnel. Her heart lifted with joy when the opening came into view. They moved deliberately, making sure no one watched as they closed the tunnel door behind them. Familiar, stuffy air surrounded them. They were safe.

Daniel took a deep breath of victory. Around him, he saw Roone the woodsman knocked out and Paulsen slowly regaining consciousness and muttering under his breath. His body weary and heavy now that the battle was done, Daniel lifted his face to feel the breeze flow across his skin, cooling and re-energizing him. Opening his eyes just a bit, he could see faces from the top of the walls leaning over and cheering him on. Their sweet sounds of laughter, joy, and merriment echoed down to him.

Prince Braden cheered especially loudly, a smile stretched across his face. The prince patted some men on the back and pointed to the excitement. It took a moment, but guards came running toward him from the castle gates, their metal armor clanking as they disarmed and tied up the two men, then ran to Daniel's side. Each man grabbed an arm and lifted him up so he was looking up the castle walls at King Theodore. King Theodore raised his fingers to his brow and nodded slightly in gratitude, their eyes locking for a moment. Daniel lowered his head in respect and smiled as feelings of relief and exhaustion rushed through him.

Daniel held on to his companions for strength as they lifted Paulsen to his feet. Daniel grabbed the back of Paulsen's arms and pushed him forward toward the gates to be led to the dungeon. Paulsen groaned as each step twisted his arms and hurt his bruised and broken bones. Chunks of mud fell off him while they made their way from the battlefield through the gates and onto the cobblestone square.

Little sympathy came from the men and women in the square as they dragged Paulsen in. They jeered at him and let their children threw stones. Those who once fled him with cries of horror now faced him with far louder shouts of condemnation.

Paulsen was thrown into the corner cell, landing with a loud thump as he hit the ground and cursed beneath his breath. The cold metal clasp of the dungeon door rang strong and clear as the door closed behind him. His cheeks were bruised blue and purple, and his eyes were still bloodshot and wild, focusing in on Daniel. Clenching his teeth together, he hissed like a caged animal. Daniel shook his head and sighed deeply, feeling relief in his heart. This creature was locked up.

Daniel turned to the guard he was leaning on.

"Where's Madeline?"

CHAPTER EIGHTEEN

The trip home through the tunnel was quicker than the trip out had been. Madeline was in a rush to return.

Entering the grand chamber where all the tunnels met, she felt a rush of wonder roll over her again. The magic of this room filled her heart. She memorized the exquisite designs on the markers. Looking around and treasuring the grandeur of the chamber for a moment, she closed her eyes and took a deep breath before choosing the tunnel marked by a castle.

The wooden door between the tunnel and the dungeon clanked loudly as they opened it. Princess Madeline stepped forward, pressing the door open with force, and practically ran into Daniel, who stood there with his mouth wide open in surprise.

"Madeline?" Daniel asked.

"Daniel, you're all right! They told me you were fighting Prince Paulsen, and I—"

Rushing to her, he picked her up and twirled her around. "What are you doing here? And what is that?" he asked, pointing to their tunnel.

"I can explain all that later," she said looking up into his eyes and tenderly moving a strand of hair out of his face.

"Don't worry, we have Paulsen locked up down

here. Your father and most of the knights are off in the forest, looking for you."

"I know. I was there when the battle started between our knights and Paulsen's men. But Emmett and his brothers were there to whisk me away." She gestured to the three figures that had just emerged from the tunnel. "But we're safe now; that's all that matters."

"Yes, we are," Daniel said, bending down for a kiss. His fingers traced the outline of her chin as their lips touched.

"Oh, please," they heard from behind them.

Turning, they saw Prince Paulsen leaning on the cell doors.

"You two make me sick," he said, snarling at them through the bars. "I cleared the forest. I fought for her. She is mine, my prize," he said, his lips turned up in a strange smile, banging his fists on the door.

Princess Madeline's stomach tightened. Daniel reached for his sword, but Madeline touched his hand and shook her head. She straightened her back and looked at the prisoner with pity. "I am not a prize, Prince Paulsen. I am a person with thoughts, feelings, and dreams. I am not something to claim, and I am most certainly not yours."

Turning her back on him, she felt better. The final weight of the battle lifted off her shoulders. She looked down and entwined her fingers with Daniel's. Beaming, they walked up the stairs together and closed the doors with a slam, feeling the dungeon door—and the past—close.

Prince Braden and King Theodore focused their eyes on the tree line. Their knights had gone in full force for battle, their horses running, banners waving, and armor clanging.

King Theodore and Prince Braden watched the horizon for movement. The sun crawled across the sky, melting the built-up snow into slush. Their breath cramped in their chests, and their fingers were white from gripping the edge of the wall. Sweat dripped down furrowed brows as they waited for a sign.

Today had been a trying day for the king, and he was anxious for news of this last stage of battle. Price Paulsen was now securely imprisoned in the dungeon. King Theodore had seen, with happy tears in his eyes, Madeline reappear with Daniel from the dungeon. Daniel had again proven himself worthy of his position and shown his love for Princess Madeline. Today was coming full circle; now he just needed news from the battlefield.

Prince Braden saw them first, the red dragons on the banners flying through the air. Victorious cheers erupted from the wooded edges. Their men were returning! Victory was secured. King Theodore clapped his hands together and smiled as he looked over his kingdom and saw hope returning to all the faces below.

The air filled with lightness as a new surge of energy erupted and cheers rang out. From the woods to the top of the towers and below in the square, everyone was celebrating. Musicians ran for their instruments. The gates creaked open to allow them through. Children danced while the women cheered and blew kisses. Laughter, music, and joy filled the air.

CHAPTER NINETEEN

Triumphant cheers echoed through the courtyard. The sunset matched the castle as every shade of red, orange, and yellow proudly flashed through the air, nature waving its own banner of victory. The air smelled tangy, a sweet mixture of the wine and the happy tears of those below. Warmth filled the hearts of those dancing in honor of their knights, their kingdom, and their freedom, and the cool breeze kept the air light and fresh. Faces beamed with smiles that had not been seen in many days.

King Theodore stood at the front of the castle walls, overseeing the commotion below. He watched over his kingdom, happiness glowing on his face. His fingers gently rubbed his chin, and a smile played at both ends of his mouth as his eyes twinkled in the sunset. His crimson robe shone as a bright beacon, the light of freedom for those dancing. Clapping his hands in rhythm to the drums, he welcomed Elias to his side.

"Elias," the king bellowed, clapping him on the shoulder and pointing to the crowd below. "Today marks a good day."

"A very good day indeed," Elias said, his smile growing as the laughter and merriment flowed through the air. His green robe blew gently behind him, sparkling in the wind.

"I think it is time, Elias. I think it is time to look at what happened and where we go from here," King Theodore said, his voice catching slightly as the emotions of the past mixed with the emotions of the day.

Both men were silent, listening to the music in the air and watching the dancers, taking their time to find the right words.

Elias looked at King Theodore. "I think our problem grew from the way we perceived events. The way you saw and felt was valid, the way I saw was valid, but perspectives are unique to each person. Look out here in the courtyard. To those dancers twirling, everything around them seems to stand still. When you stop and step back and observe, as we are, you can see the movement all around. The dancers, the banners waving, the children playing, even the wind blowing. Everything is in constant flow. Depending on your perspective, your focus, sometimes small—or even large—pieces can be missed." Elias's eyes shone.

King Theodore rubbed his chin, taking in everything he had heard. His eyes were soft, his cheeks warm and red, and with an outstretched arm, he looked at Elias and smiled. "All is forgiven. All is well to move forward from here."

"That we will, for Eleanor," Elias said with a strong grasp of his arm.

"For Eleanor," King Theodore agreed. They embraced, and years of worry, tears, fear and anger disappeared in their arms.

"Father," Prince Braden said, approaching the two men, kneeling to the ground.

"Son, rise," the king said. "This is a time of celebration; no formalities are needed." King Theodore grasped his son's hand and smiled.

Braden smiled in return but kept his face veiled. "Father, the last few days have made something very clear to me. I chose to follow you, and these past few days have shown all that I still need to work toward. I vow to you my pledge of duty, honor, and respect."

Braden looked up at his father, hope glistening in his eyes, devotion evident in his set jaw. His father grasped his hand and pulled him in for a hug.

Elias smiled and his heart grew as he watched his kinsmen reconnect. Beyond their shoulders, Elias caught a glimpse of red dashing out of view. Excusing himself, he ran down the stairs to follow her. Her sobs were easy to track as they wound their way around the crowd. When he found her, she lay on the ground with her head in her hands and her red hair swept to the side. Her pale skin glowed beneath the sunset sky.

"My dear Sophia," Elias said, patting her back. "I take it you heard the prince?" he asked, helping her to a standing position. She mutely nodded, trying to calm her trembling chin, sniffling to stop the tears from flowing. Looking up at Elias, she sought his eyes.

"He pledged his life to duty. Where does that leave me?" she asked, her eyes imploring an answer that Elias could not give. "I am a noble beneath his rank. I openly defied the king and helped the princess do so as well. I don't even know who I am, where I belong." She looked at him, pleading for something to give her hope.

Elias squeezed her hand. "We all walk a different path. Sometimes that keeps us together, sometimes it sets us apart, allowing growth or change. I cannot tell you where to look, but I can attest that there is strength in you that you don't see yet. A magic waiting to be unveiled." He looked at her deeply for a moment before closing his eyes. The wind blew through their hair.

"Yes," he said with a smile, "definitely magic waiting to be discovered." Elias patted her on her shoulder and laughed whimsically as he returned to the king's side.

Biting her lip, she tilted her head, watching him walk away, wondering what it was that he saw. Her eyes followed him back to the edge of the stairs and settled back on Braden, who stood elbow to elbow with the king.

"Excuse me, Sophia?" came a quiet voice next to her. She turned, her hair whipping around.

Emmett smiled at her sweetly, almost shyly, holding his hand out. "It's a celebration. Would you join me for a dance?" he asked, his eyes showing hope and nervousness.

Sophia took a deep breath and stole a quick glance behind her at Braden. Turning back to Emmett, she flashed her biggest smile.

"Yes, it is a celebration," she said, taking his hand and lifting the hem of her skirt. They ran to the center of the square to join the fun, their laughter joining the festive around them.

Princess Madeline sat on the edge of the fountain, leaning back into Daniel's arms. Snuggling in, she felt the tingles settle into her stomach and smiled, knowing she was safe and home with her knight. Her fingers traced his as their hands entwined.

"Daniel?" she asked, looking up at him, her emerald eyes searching his face.

"Hmm?"

"Are we safe now? Where do we go from here?"

"There's only one place to go from here, my princess. We move forward."

"Where is that?" she asked, seeing secrecy in his eyes.

Letting go of her hands, he turned her so she was facing him, their eyes locked onto each other. "We go back to Dragon's Gate." His eyes twinkled as a smile grew on her face. "I have a team ready to go, we just need your father's approval before we set out."

"But how? How did you plan all this?"

"Madeline, you're in my thoughts all the time. My future is by your side. It is my job, my goal to help make all your dreams come true."

"All my dreams have come true," Madeline said, leaning toward him, pulling him close for a tender kiss. Their lips locked as the music rose around them. Tonight was a dream come true for all.

EPILOGUE—DRAGON'S GATE

The seasons turned quicker in the north, and it wasn't long before spring knocked on its door. The winter snows had begun to melt. Vibrant greens from the forest contrasted against the skies, and the rich, dark earth blossomed as the snow retreated. Beautiful wildflowers in every color sprouted around them like scattered jewels, bright visions of treasure laced within the ground.

Princess Madeline smiled, taking in new smells. A spicy aroma hung in the air, tantalizing her senses, lilac and perhaps mint. Her horse snorted. She patted him gently before dismounting.

Her feet sank into the muddy ground, the bottom of her riding boots now dirty, but Madeline did not mind. Spinning around with excitement, she raised her head to the sky and smiled as the sun found a way to shine down on her.

"What do you think, Madeline?" Daniel asked with a smile, brushing his hair out of his face.

"Oh, Daniel," she said, throwing her arms over his shoulders. "I think we've found our home." She spun around to see more.

The landscape rolled in gentle hills, allowing for good vantage points. To the south, she could see the tree line of the great forest; the western plains rolled out before her in long waves, and the eastern flats looked as barren as they did from where she had grown up. Her eyes glistened as she looked north. Dragon's Gate stood in front of her, its high archway welcoming her as it had on the first day.

She recalled how the sun had appeared to wink at her from under the red archway that day. Today she felt the full scrutiny of the gate's eye. She could see the trepidation in the eyes of a few members of her group as they glanced up, perhaps recalling childhood stories of dragons. For her, there was no fear, only a deep, growing fire inside.

She knew, standing with the wind blowing in her face, that she was home.

"I can see it now," she said, smiling. "Our castle here, the stables down there." She pointed down the rolling valley. "You can have your tournament field there. And the gardens, we must have gardens," she said wistfully, already lost in thought. The possibilities were limitless as they imagined their future together. Something in the sky caught her eye, growing closer and larger.

"Daniel?" she asked, pulling him near. "What kind of bird is that?"

Squinting his eyes, Daniel looked up toward the sky. "Not any I have ever seen. Men, come quick," he said, motioning behind him to the other guards. "That, in the sky, have any of you seen it before?"

The men all squinted, looking up at the approaching bird in wonder. The animal seemed to grow larger with each wave of its wings, undulating through the clouds as if swimming through waves.

The group watched, transfixed on the animal, and Elias approached to look. With astonishment, he jerked his eyes open, furrowing his brow. "That is no bird, Princess. Take cover!" Elias ran, hastily grabbing Madeline's wrist and pulling her away.

"Elias, wait," she said, trying to free her arm. "What is going on?" she asked, rubbing her wrist where he had pulled it.

"Princess, it's a dragon."

The dragon appeared above their heads, larger and quicker than before. Its dark green body undulated through the sky, the scales on its body shimmering in the sunlight. Its wings expanded over the length of a tournament field.

"Daniel!" she screamed, running as quickly as she could back to their horses, trying to find cover in the landscape. There wasn't much to hide behind in this territory. The trees were low and spread out.

The men had all scattered as far as they could run. Elias camouflaged into the bushes with his green robe; some of the guards were already galloping off on horseback. Daniel raced toward Madeline, sweat beading on his temples. Without thinking, he grabbed her around the waist and threw her over his shoulder, running as fast as he could to any shelter. Her dress swept in front of his face and her chest heaved into his back as the fear pounded through them both. He squatted down low and brought Madeline to the ground below him to protect her from attack.

"Where did you take us?" she asked, feeling the smooth rock beneath her. "Are we inside?" she asked, her voice trembling.

"Dragon's Gate," he finished.

The wings beat faster and louder as the dragon approached, the force of the wind pushing them deeper into the rocks. Madeline took a deep breath, then gasped in horror when the dragon lurched toward them. "No!" she yelled with all her might, squeezing her hand around her shell necklace. Reflective rainbows seemed to flicker off the shell onto the smooth rock around them, and warmth radiated through her palm. Her body shuddered twice before falling limp. The dragon swooped beneath Dragon's Gate, right above their heads before moving north.

Once they were sure it had moved on, the other knights rushed to their side. Daniel knelt beside Madeline, fanning her face with his hands, tears in his eyes, willing her to wake up. The other guards gave him a respectful distance, taking turns scanning the sky.

Elias stood to the side, rubbing his chin, raising his face to the wind. The dragons had been gone for hundreds of years. What could have brought them back? No answers came to him, but he had a feeling this was just the beginning.

ABOUT THE AUTHOR

Kirstin Pulioff is a storyteller at heart. Born and raised in Southern California, she moved to the Pacific Northwest to follow her dreams and graduated from Oregon State University with a degree in Forest Management. Happily married and a mother of two, she lives in the foothills of Colorado. When she's not writing an adventure, she's busy living one.

Website: www.kirstinpulioff.com
Facebook: KirstinPulioffAuthor
Twitter: @KirstinPulioff

Published Works
Middle Grade Fantasy
    The Escape of Princess Madeline
    The Battle for Princess Madeline
    The Dragon and Princess Madeline
    The Princess Madeline Trilogy (box set)

YA Fantasy
    Dreamscape: Saving Alex
Short Stories
    The Ivory Tower
    Boone's Journey

THE ESCAPE OF PRINCESS MADELINE
(Book One of the Princess Madeline series)

Madeline, princess of Soron, awakens on her sixteenth birthday to find that her father has already made preparations for her betrothal. When she disappears unexpectedly, her suitors and knight champion rush to the rescue. But all is not as it seems, and the errant princess's flight has put the kingdom at stake…

Can Madeline find freedom or does it come with too high a price?

Available in digital and print formats from most online distributors.

THE DRAGON AND PRINCESS MADELINE
(Book Three of the Princess Madeline series)

Princess Madeline is ready to celebrate. With the foundation of her future in place, it seems nothing can hurt her. Then the return of a mysterious green dragon threatens their kingdom and king. Will this challenge prove to be too much for Princess Madeline and Prince Braden, or will they find the answers they seek hidden in cryptic messages from the past?

Can Madeline save her kingdom from the dragon or is the real danger something else?

Available in digital and print formats from most online distributors.

CPSIA information can be obtained
at www.ICGtesting.com
Printed in the USA
LVHW051557080719
623451LV00018B/832/P

9 781503 213036